Great
Eagle
Wood

Published in 2008 by
Institute of Chartered Accountants in Ireland
CA House, Pembroke Road
Ballsbridge, DUBLIN 4

Illustrations by Kevin McSherry
Designed and typeset in 12 on 15.5pt Baskerville by Marsha Swan
Printed by ColourBooks, Dublin
The paper used in the printing of this book was produced from managed, renewable, plantation forests.

ISBN 978 0 903854 06 1

Great Eagle Wood

Derry Cotter

Institute of Chartered Accountants in Ireland
Dublin

To Paula, Diarmuid, Orla and John:
may all of your dreams come true

In memory of Robert

Chapter One

The breeze had stiffened, and the last of the sun's rays were barely visible, as Edgar the Eagle flapped his wings and rose effortlessly towards the Freedom Tower. A grey windowless structure at the centre of the wood, from its summit the Tower afforded a view over miles of lush woodland. Sinking his talons into its tough outer surface, Edgar blinked when a rabbit scurried homewards in what remained of the half-light. In the distance, an orange glow spread throughout the wood as fires came to life, their influence growing as darkness continued to descend.

Edgar stretched and inhaled the Great Wood deep into his lungs, knowing that tomorrow he would be leader and become a prisoner of sorts. So, uncounted and anonymous, this night was his. Startled by a movement, Edgar saw a squirrel hunt for nuts along the oak closest to the Tower. Finding one, it retraced its steps expertly and disappeared inside an opening in the tree.

That night Edgar did his best to sleep, but the more he tried the harder it became. Closing his eyes, he was forced to open them again, trying in vain to stop the thoughts that were racing in his head. He smiled as he remembered how, as a young eagle, he used to respond to his mother's scoldings.

'Wait until I'm leader of the Great Wood,' he would say, the threat never failing to win her amused forgiveness. Now, as the night lengthened, Edgar feared that the challenge would prove too great. He had been head of the Eyrie District, he reminded himself, and had served a double term in the House of Eagles. He had played a part too in furthering the rights of ravens, enslaved because of their blackness, and freed only after a bitter civil war. But would that be enough, he wondered, or would the Great Wood demand more than he would be able to give.

Edgar heard the grandfather clock in the hall strike twelve, then one and two, and then…

'Wake up, Mr Edgar! It's eight o'clock, sir.'

Edgar yawned and shielded his eyes from the sun, as Sam, his beaver assistant, opened the curtains.

'Your newspaper, sir.'

Forcing his eyes open, Edgar studied the morning's headlines before going downstairs for breakfast. Afterwards he retired to his study to read his acceptance speech yet again. Moving a pencil along the pages, he paused to draw a line through something on page one and added a comment in the margin.

'Your escort is outside, sir,' said the beaver assistant, opening the door of the study. From his desk Edgar took a last look at the photograph above the mantelpiece, knowing that his parents would have been proud of him today. Folding the pages of his speech, he rose to leave,

There was a shaking of heads in the great hall, and a badger covered his eyes at the mention of such debauchery.

'The Great Eagle's dream was of a land that would give comfort to the poor, strength to the weak and courage to the faint-hearted, a land in which every creature is created equal, regardless of species, colour or creed. The Great Eagle dreamt of justice for all, in a land where peace would prevail, with all creatures living together in harmony. He dreamt too of friendships forged with woods to the north and the south, and woods to the east and the west. In His own immortal words, "All woods are good".'

Edgar paused as the hall filled with the sound of the Great Eagle's mantra, the two pews of beavers at the back being the most vocal of all.

'All woods are good. All woods are good. All woods are good...'

It was almost two minutes before Edgar was able to continue.

'The land of which the Great Eagle spoke is a good land, a land of principles and ideals, where the rivers and trees provide nourishment and creatures care for one another in good times and in bad. Long ago, Creege and Emor boasted woods which, though great, eventually went into decline. Great Eagle Wood will surpass all of that and everything that has gone before. Here, creatures will live together in freedom, accomplish great deeds and lead the free woods in a spirit of peace and in the image of the Great Eagle.'

There was tumultuous applause, which continued for several minutes and ended only when the beavers grew tired of reciting 'The Great Wood is great'. Edgar continued, pointing skywards towards the giant statue.

'The torch so nobly lit by our munificent founder, the

Great Eagle, has been passed in turn to each generation who answered His call. That flame has been nurtured and nourished, and it glows today more brightly than ever before. Now the torch of destiny has passed into our hands, and it is our duty to accomplish great deeds of liberty and freedom and to pass our legacy to those who follow us. I, Edgar, pledge myself to fulfilling the dream of the Great Eagle. Together, and in His image, there is no limit to what we can achieve.'

The audience rose as one and began to shout Edgar's name. The noise level now exceeded all that had gone before and it continued until the ram, fearing for the crowd's safety, approached the rostrum and appealed for calm. Eventually the crowd drifted away, leaving the beavers alone in the Great Hall, their chants alternating between 'Edgar, Edgar' and 'The Great Wood is great'.

Outside, Edgar was already on his way, flying under the protection of the falcons as they steered a course for his new home. Below them animals waved excitedly, eager to show their approval of the new leader. Looking down, Edgar smiled and waved too, and as the falcon convoy veered left he knew that he would remember this moment forever.

PILLOWS for SALE
McSherry

Chapter Two

Edgar spent his first week in office with a constant stream of advisers camped on his doorstep. Although official business was given priority, more mundane issues had to be dealt with too, such as cutting the tape at a school opening and being the celebrity eagle at a charity fete. On Tuesday he received a delegation from the females' association, before attending the funeral of a goose who crashed while attempting to set a Great Wood land speed record. Later in the week he was guest of honour at an old-timers' reunion, and he went walkabout on Friday, meeting residents on the east of the wood. There he discovered the risk involved in patting porcupines, as doting mothers jostled their offspring to the front of the queue. Even trickier was having to kiss babies, with the skunks having, at best, a patchy understanding of such formalities.

On Wednesday of week two Edgar paid a nostalgic visit to the River Bank. Landing on an oak tree, he dislodged an acorn, which dropped to the ground and rolled towards the river's edge. Catching the down slope, it entered the water to join a myriad of flora, mostly of green and brown. Edgar felt his skin tingle, remembering it was here that his father had come to save for a young eagle's education, thus sowing the seeds of high office. Edgar sensed that he was watching now, and he felt proud that his father's sacrifice had been worthwhile.

Some said the loss would fade with time, but now, as leader, Edgar missed him more than ever. Sometimes, it was the advice he had so highly valued, or an insight that made him look again, and differently. Other times, it was a word of kindness, a comforting shoulder, or a twinkle in his eye.

'Are you looking for the rat?'

Startled by the question, Edgar turned towards the voice and saw two swans floating in the water.

'Are you looking for the rat?' they asked again, both talking but appearing to share the one voice.

'Yes, actually I am,' replied Edgar, not wanting them to think otherwise.

'He's over there.'

Edgar stared along a pole, towards the centre of the river, and saw a figure disappear into a vault. He emerged a moment later and stood on the pole, sniffing the air.

'Hello, rat,' said Edgar, waving to attract his attention.

'Oh, it's you, Edgar.'

'Just making a courtesy call. Nothing official, you understand.'

'Well, I'm a bit busy, but seeing as you're here…'

It was typical of the rat, thought Edgar, as he accepted the reluctant invitation to tea. Making you feel as welcome as was necessary, he would talk only about his bank. His father had been the same, it was said, and his grandfather even more so. Nonetheless, as an important provider of finance, the rat had to be indulged as much as one could stomach.

On his return home, Edgar rested on an oak to break his journey. Below him, on the ground, he noticed a homemade billboard advertising 'Pillows for Sale'.

'Not like that,' screamed a duck called Bill, spitting feathers from his mouth as his son let a bag slip from his grasp.

'How many times do I have to tell you? Ducks don't have hands, so you've just got to get on with it!'

'Yes, Dad,' replied the duckling, lowering his head to retrieve the bag from the ground.

A badger family approached in the distance, and Bill's mood lifted, the prospect of a sale wiping the scowl from his face.

'Best down in town,' he boasted, the worn sales line drawing a yawn from his thinly coated son.

The badgers stopped in front of Bill, and as the youngsters played on their father's back their mother got straight to the point.

'How much for the large pillows?' she enquired, opening her purse and closing it again.

'Half price today,' said the duck, his face lighting up in anticipation of a sale.

'They were half price yesterday,' complained the badger, beckoning to her family as she turned to leave. Dropping a partly filled pillow, the duck took two full ones from a greyish holdall.

‘Four for two,’ he shouted, beaming broadly when the departing badger turned her head.

‘Two small ones free with two adult pillows. You won’t do better than that.’

The badger stood, motionless, her demeanour offering no clue as to whether she would leave or stay. Steadying the youngsters on his back, her mate whispered in her ear and she re-opened negotiations with the duck.

‘What about pillowcases?’ she enquired expectantly.

This time it was the duck who paused fleetingly, before thrusting his head into the holdall and emerging with four pillowcases in his bill.

‘Okay, okay! You drive a hard bargain, madam. But a sale is a sale. I’ll throw them in with the pillows. Is that an offer or what?’

High on the oak, Edgar the Eagle watched the duck wrap his produce in brown paper as the badger rummaged in her purse. Such deals, he thought, were what made the Great Wood what it was. Tonight, the badger family would nestle together more snugly than they had ever nestled before. The father would praise his mate for bargaining so astutely, while she would take pride in the comfort of their home. Next month, they would put some more of their savings aside and maybe buy something for downstairs.

Satisfied with his work, the duck collected the unsold pillows and began to lecture his son on the art of selling.

‘The customer is king. Never forget that, son. Got it?’

The youngster nodded his head repeatedly, knowing it was his best chance of being allowed to go home.

'If the customer says it's black, it's black. White and it's white. Got it, son?'

'The customer is king, isn't that it, Dad?'

'That's my boy,' said the duck, continuing to talk shop as they walked the short distance home.

Edgar was proud of what he had seen. A master of his craft, every sale mattered to the duck called Bill. Tonight, in the Great Wood, pillow talk would be the hottest topic of all, and tomorrow that badger family would send four, maybe five customers seeking his wares. Most importantly of all, thought Edgar, the skill of the master was being handed on, and in time the young duck would inherit his father's business and nurture it anew.

The opening of the wood's first pillow shop by the duck called Bill was the highlight of Edgar's early days in office. It was a proud duck who posed with his family at the official opening, attended by one of the largest crowds seen in the wood. Edgar was guest of honour, and there was a hush as he stood on the rostrum of a specially constructed stage.

'My friends, the new shop you see before you is one of the finest in Great Eagle Wood. No expense has been spared, and its design is of the highest architectural standards. I congratulate the Beaver Construction Team, whose dedication and attention to detail is second to none. There exists no finer group of workers in this wood or in any other.'

Edgar paused as the beavers cheered loudly and began to chant.

'Beavers are best, beavers are best…'

Eventually, he was allowed to continue.

'We must thank too our friends in the East Wood, who hired out the diggers, and our friends in the West Wood, who supplied the glass for the windows.'

His next comments were drowned out as the beavers began to chant once again.

'All woods are good, all woods are good…'

'We acknowledge also,' continued Edgar, 'the immense contribution of the River Bank, without whose funding none of this would have been possible.'

Pausing for the applause, Edgar took off his reading glasses and put his notes to one side.

'Behind this fine building, my friends, lies a duck, a duck with a vision that this Great Wood should bring peace and prosperity to all. Bill has risked everything and, thanks to him, in the nights to come every animal will rest his head on a pillow unsurpassed for comfort and quality. Standing beside him today is his family, whose love and support have provided help and sustenance in times of adversity. On your behalf, I would like to present this bouquet to his partner Lucy as a gesture of our appreciation.'

The crowd rose to applaud, and Lucy smiled shyly as she accepted the flowers. Returning to the rostrum, Edgar waited until the noise had died down before continuing.

'Long ago the Great Eagle lit the flame of freedom in this wood. Today, Bill has ensured that same flame continues to burn brightly. For as long as we possess the courage and fortitude shown by this duck, we need never fear for the future of our great wood. My friends, I now declare this shop open for business, and I ask the Great Eagle to watch over it in the years ahead.'

Amid deafening applause Edgar cut the tape and stepped to the safety of the security cordon as the crowd surged forward.

Later that spring, Edgar reached middle age in good health, his seven thousand feathers as strong and smooth as they were in his prime. He had fathered two daughters, and though he had craved a son it was not to be. Now, as he awaited the birth of his first grandson, Edgar was thankful for a second chance.

The eagle would be born on the night of a new moon, said a ram who studied the stars and whose views were widely respected. And so the full white gave way and was half, before fading towards crescent and then nothing. On the night of the new moon, the ram foretold of a great event.

'Tonight, an eagle will come who will one day lead the wood at a time of great need. This one, like the eagles of old, will talk to the wind and the sky.'

The words of the ram spread, and throughout the wood animals searched the sky for news. Ten o'clock came, then eleven, and as midnight approached some began to question the ram's predictions. On the stroke of twelve, there was a clatter of wings and a team of falcons rose from their station to announce the new arrival. The animals celebrated, their cheers releasing the tension that had gripped the Great Wood. Then came the news that the eagle was to be called Abby, and the cheers stopped as suddenly as they had begun.

'The great leader is a female!' scoffed a badger. 'Whoever heard of a female leader?'

'He's a fraud,' shouted a beaver. 'Why, that ram should be locked up!'

Away from it all, Edgar stood perched on top of the Freedom Tower, where he had gone to be alone. Once again he had been denied an heir, and he shivered a little as the trees shifted in the wind. Then, knowing that every life was precious, he stared into the night sky and resolved to accept what the Great Eagle had ordained.

Edgar felt a weight lift from his shoulders, and though the wind had risen he no longer felt its chill. Above him, he spotted a shooting star, and he followed it across the sky, wishing for his granddaughter a life of fulfilment. Higher up, amid the Great Bear that is Ursa Major, he saw the Plough, its shape doubling as a cradle for the newborn eagle. It was some constellation, and Edgar smiled.

BOB'S
FLYING
SCHOOL
BFS

Chapter Three

That December, the youngsters of Great Eagle Wood danced about excitedly as pieces of the moon seemed to fall from the sky.

'Look at me, Mum,' boasted a squirrel, jumping from branch to branch and cutting off the flow of white crystals before they could settle on his tree-house.

'That's snow,' explained his mother patiently. 'It comes when the rain freezes and turns into soft pieces of ice.'

'Snow! Did ya hear that, guys? Mum says it's snow. Isn't that cool?'

The next morning, a blanket of white covered the rooftops and triangular tree peaks stretched skywards, grasping for light. On the ground, youngsters pestered their mothers for pieces of coal and made eyes for their snow creatures, which stared impassively as home-made sleighs trundled up and down the slopes of Great Eagle Wood.

December, as always, came and went, but the white visitor stayed, his influence reduced by daytime shovelling,

like a squirrel. The beavers of Chestnut Hill searched the deepest recesses of their memories, but nobody could recall a beaver ever wanting to be like a duck before.

Beryl was worried that if she challenged him Bob would deny it, which would make matters worse. Yet, with his behaviour growing increasingly strange, she knew it was an issue that she could not duck forever. On Saturday she lit a fire, cooked a special meal and served up Bob's favourite rice dish for dessert.

'You know, Bob, I've been thinking,' she began.

'Yes, love?'

'If you want to change…'

'Change?'

'Sometimes a beaver might want to try something different. Maybe to be like someone else.'

'Like someone else?'

'It's okay with me, really it is.'

'What's okay, love?'

'If you want to be like a duck, Bob. It's okay with me.'

Beryl bit her lip as Bob fell silent. A tear trickled from his eye as he thought about the duck called Bill – how he had started with nothing and built up such a successful business. It was because ducks were so good at selling. 'Two for one, one for free, half price today,' would be his opening offer. Then, once he had grabbed everyone's interest, he'd throw in a pillow case and, if that didn't seal the deal, maybe a lace handkerchief. Hopping from foot to foot, he would warn of shortages, talk of changing fashions and describe the softness of his pillows. They almost always bought, rarely out of need and more often because they had fallen under his spell. Then, convinced they had got a bargain, they would rush to hand over the money, fearing a change of mind.

Bob had wanted for so long to start his own business, yet it came as a shock to hear someone say it.

'Are you sure?' he asked her.

'Sure about what?' said Beryl, her eyes filling up at the sight of Bob's tear-stained face.

'About me wanting to be like a duck. Are you sure you don't mind?'

'Come here to me!'

Beryl held Bob close and felt her head start to spin. Beavers were beavers, and as far as she was concerned there was no need to be anything else. They did their work, received a fair wage and left ducks to do the thinking. Why Bob would want to start his own business she had no idea, but she had made up her mind that she would give him all the support he needed. Beryl closed her eyes, and as Bob melted into his mate's embrace he felt the weight of the wood lift off his shoulders. Now that his secret was out, he wondered why he hadn't confided in Beryl in the first place.

'It's just that they're so good at business, Beryl. Ducks always seem to know what will sell. That's the reason I want to be like them.'

'Do you think you *can* be like them, Bob?'

'I don't know, Beryl. But I'm going to give it a try. '

Bob was determined to succeed, and things soon began to fall into place. He was warmly received at the ducks' monthly business dinner, and an invitation to tea from the duck called Bill was an unexpected bonus. On the appointed day, Bob rushed about the house getting ready. Having checked himself in the mirror, he pecked Beryl on the cheek, quipped

'Time is money,' and disappeared in the direction of Bill's house. In no time at all he had put Chestnut Hill behind him and soon passed through Mandarin Drive, leading to even larger dwellings on Barbary Avenue. There, he easily located number 7 and knocked on the door, which was slightly ajar.

'Ah, Bob, come on in,' said Bill from the dining room.

'Hi Bill, thanks,' replied Bob

'Pull up a chair by the fire. There's still a chill, I can feel it in my bones. Cup o' tea?'

'Yes, please.'

'Great to see ya at the business dinner, Bob. It's good that yer thinkin' about business potential. If ya want to make money, seein' the wood from the trees is what's important.'

Bob nodded and smiled, but the truth was that he was still seeing trees. He knew there was a wood out there somewhere, but he couldn't quite get his head around it. Still, if Bill said it was there, that was good enough for him.

'Why, there are opportunities everywhere in this wood, Bob. Once ya spot 'em, yer on yer way to the first million. Now that yer seein' things like a duck, gettin' rich is only a matter o' time.'

'So what do I need to do?'

'Ya must think of somethin' that a lot of animals do, Bob. Take sleepin'. There's nothin' moves in this wood that doesn't sleep. An' what do animals need when they sleep? I'll tell ya,' said Bill, starting to salivate at the gem he was about to reveal. 'Pillows! That's what. An' the more they sleep, the more pillows they need!'

Bob nodded, but he didn't know why. He used just one pillow himself, no matter how long he slept for. In fact, the only time he used a second one was when he was reading. Sometimes, when Beryl was using their spare pillow, he'd put a book under his head instead. One night, he put his head on the book that he intended to read and he ended up just falling asleep.

'Walkin' is the same, Bob. Nearly everyone around here walks. So what do they need? You tell me.'

Bob stared into space, which is what he did when he wanted to think. He usually had everything he needed when he went walking, unless it started to rain and he had forgotten to bring his hat.

'I'll tell ya. It's shoes. That's what ya need for walkin'. Got it, Bob? Now that yer startin' to see things clearly, pretty soon you'll have yer own business. Just ya wait an' see.'

Bob emerged, rubbing his hands, from Bill's house. If making money was so easy, he thought, why, pretty much anyone could do it. All you needed was to think of something that a lot of animals do. Or was it something that some animals did a lot? Bob racked his brain, and then he racked it some more. He didn't sleep that night, or the night after, or the night after that. By Friday, his head was overheating and Beryl was concerned.

'What's the matter, Bob? You've been pacing the floor ever since your lunch with that duck.'

'I need to think of something, Beryl. Something that everyone does. Like walking or sleeping.'

'Sleeping? Everyone does that except you. And walking? You're doing enough of that, anyway!'

Bob sighed aloud and covered his head.

'What about flying?' added Beryl. 'It's faster than walking and it's fine unless you're afraid of heights.'

'What?'

'I said flying is for the birds.'

Beryl was right, thought Bob, as he stared into space. Most birds did fly, at least the ones that *he* knew anyway. And they did it often, too, which was even better. Some flew faster, some lower or higher, but they all flew. Small birds seemed to fly short distances, while larger ones could keep going all day. Or was it the other way around, he wondered, because the heavier their wings the faster they got tired.

Suddenly a gem of an idea penetrated Bob's brain, and he began to twirl Beryl around the kitchen.

'You're making me dizzy, Bob. Stop!'

'We're going to be rich, Beryl! I'm a genius. Wait 'til Bill finds out.'

The suspense began to build on Chestnut Hill as the day of Bob's business launch drew near. Posters made from pillow bags hung from trees, marking time, and with seven days to go, beavers were stopping on the street to exchange views.

'It's something to do with construction,' said one.

'That's what Bob knows best,' agreed a second.

'I think he's going to start making pillows,' guessed a third.

'And go into competition with the duck called Bill? No chance!'

Bob was revealing nothing, not even to Beryl, who found herself alternating between a state of anxiety and feverish curiosity. Finally the day arrived, and a huge crowd assembled at the clearing. Mostly it was beavers who packed the enclosure, their appetites whetted by the tree posters' daily countdown, but two rows of chairs reserved for ducks were full as well. Overhead, a giant banner hung between two oak trees, its letters concealed under a blanket of leaves. Underneath the banner, the duck called Bill, who was master of ceremonies, was standing on a makeshift podium.

'My friends,' began Bill.

'We have among us a beaver who has spared nothin' in gettin' his new business up and runnin'. For my part, I am proud that we have welcomed Bob as one of our own, and today he becomes as much a duck as us ducks ourselves. So c'mon, show yer appreciation right now.'

The enclosure came alive with sustained clapping, the armless ducks nodding their heads and smiling broadly.

'Now, my friends,' continued Bill, 'the great moment has arrived.'

Beryl held her breath as Bob walked to the nearby oak. Reaching on tiptoe, he caught a rope cord and began to pull downwards. Overhead, the blanket of leaves was drawn back, and animals stared skywards as the giant banner was unmasked letter by letter.

'F-l-y-i-n-g S-c-h-o-o-l' came into view, and the ducks in the front row nodded approvingly.

'F-o-r' emerged on the right-hand side of the banner, and everyone waited in anticipation for the final section to appear. Leaning backwards, Bob pulled hard on the cord but it resisted stubbornly, and two beavers stepped forward, forming a tug-of-war team with Bob at the rear. The strain showed on their faces as they tested the rope, which continued to defy them. Then, on a count of three, they pulled together and there was a ripping sound as the leaf blanket came away.

'Flying School for Birds' boasted the banner, now peeled

from its leafy cover and battling vigorously against the breeze. There was silence for a moment before the assembly of beavers broke into sustained applause, shouting 'Bob, Bob, Bob…' Up on the podium, Bill stared open-mouthed, and the two rows of ducks were doubled up laughing.

Later, when they were alone, Beryl confessed to having been worried about the launch.

'I'm not sure, Bob…'

'We're going to be rich, Beryl! Did you see how happy the ducks were?'

'But one of them was saying…'

'The River Bank is so impressed, they're giving us a loan.'

'They are?'

'We just have to sign this form.'

'It's all about our cottage, Bob,' said Beryl, trying to make sense of the loan agreement.

'Who cares, Beryl? We'll have enough money to buy ten cottages!'

Bob immediately began the search for a flying instructor, quickly eliminating four toads with a fear of heights and a bullfrog who suffered from travel sickness. He whittled a shortlist of six down to three, deciding eventually on an owl who claimed to be an expert in mind games. The following Monday the flying school opened for business, and first up was a migrating swallow, who took advice on endurance flights and disappeared without paying. A flock of magpies was next, enquiring about the latest in dive-bombing techniques. Tuesday was quiet, as was the remainder of the week, and on Friday the owl passed the time trying to interest some crows in a course of singing lessons.

The rat paid a visit in week two, and expressed concern about the lack of customers. The school needed to make a lodgement, he said, and he would be expecting to see them at the River Bank. Bob nodded, offering as much reassurance as the rat was willing to listen to.

Unfortunately, things were no better the following week, or the week after that.

'This isn't working,' said Bob in week four. 'All the birds can fly already.'

'So what are we going to do?' asked the owl.

'We need to come up with something new,' said Bob.

'Yeah, but what?'

'I don't know.'

'Maybe we should teach turkeys how to fly,' suggested the owl.

'Turkeys can't fly!' said Bob.

'Exactly.'

Bob scratched his chin and stared into space. Surely turkeys would fly if they could, he thought. Then again, what if they had never tried? What if generations of turkeys had been grounded, unaware that they could fly? One thing was certain – if the school was to survive it needed paying customers, and, if the owl was right, this could be the breakthrough they had been waiting for.

The following day Bob accompanied the owl to Turkey Mountain, where they hoped to enlist a volunteer. Flying was a question of confidence, explained the owl, putting his proposal to a small crowd of onlookers. Turkeys had been misinformed, he said, and had yet to fulfil their potential. What use were wings, he asked, if you didn't use them to fly. With that, the owl suddenly rose into the air and continued to talk, hovering barely high enough to stay airborne.

'It's easy,' he said. 'Anyone can fly if he wants to. Why, that beaver over there could do it, and he doesn't even have wings.'

The turkeys stared at Bob, who smiled and began to make flapping movements with his shoulders.

'You see? You just have to believe that you can do it,' continued the owl. 'Now, who wants to become the first turkey to reach the sky?'

Sucked in by the impressive sales pitch, several males surged forward, vying for the opportunity. Bob conferred with the owl and they eventually decided on the turkey who looked to be least attached to the ground. A date was set for the flight, and they departed, promising to return triumphantly with the selected bird.

The following Thursday, the owl led the portly turkey to a cliff edge, and Bob watched as he tried to cajole the reluctant fowl into jumping off.

'I can't do it!' pleaded the turkey, nervously backing away from the edge.

'You can fly if you believe,' said the owl.

'I can't!'

'You can if I say you can,' insisted the owl. 'Now repeat after me: I can fly, I can fly.'

'I can fly, I can fly,' gabbled the turkey, staring into the depths of the unfathomable gorge.

'You can if you believe you can,' affirmed the owl.

'I can fly, I can fly,' repeated the turkey, and trundling forward in a trance, he launched himself into the gorge.

Bob held his breath as the turkey stayed level with the ledge, his wings outdoing themselves to stay airborne.

'You can fly,' insisted the owl, treading air alongside and staring deep into the turkey's eyes.

Bob watched with growing concern as the turkey's wings began to tire under the strain. Gabbling incoherently, he made a sudden lunge for the safety of the ledge, but managed only to collide with the rock face underneath.

'You can fly,' insisted the owl, moving swiftly aside as the flailing turkey tried to grab onto him for support.

The turkey's cries echoed through the gorge as he plummeted downwards, leaving a scattering of feathers floating in his wake. Back on the ledge, the owl absolved himself of blame.

'If only he had believed,' he said gravely.

The turkey's disappearance triggered rumours of unnatural practices at the flying school, and as customer numbers dwindled to nothing, the fledgling business was forced to close.

Beryl took the news badly. The ducks' reaction on the day of the launch had worried her but she had tried to be optimistic for Bob's sake. Now, as she fretted about the future,

Bob was already on the lookout for the next opportunity. Intent on having his own business, he devoted all his time to staring into space until he came up with a new idea.

'It's a dead cert, Beryl. Why, they do it all the time. Every one of them.'

'Who does what?'

'Fish. All they do is swim.'

'So?'

'So they need a swimming school, of course,' smiled Bob.

'Are you sure, Bob? Maybe you should ask someone…'

'Of course I'm sure, Beryl! Am I smart or what?'

Bob sank everything he had into his new venture. In the first week they helped a plaice to find his bearings and coached a turbot who was determined to swim faster. The owl, who had been retained as an instructor, came up with a ground-breaking theory to pass the time.

'A dogfish, being half-animal, should spend half its time on land.'

Bob shrugged his shoulders as the owl coaxed a reluctant dogfish from the water and stared deep into his eyes.

'You can breathe if you believe,' insisted the owl. 'Repeat after me: I can breathe, I can breathe.'

'I can breathe, I can breathe,' gasped the dogfish, his tail beating the ground as he began to thrash about frantically.

'You can breathe if you believe you can,' insisted the owl, interpreting the rapid movements as a good sign.

Gradually the dogfish's struggle faded, and a minute later he lay motionless, his mouth open, facing the sky.

'He didn't believe,' said the owl sadly.

Amid undercurrents of resentment, the swimming school for fish went under, and the authorities launched an inquiry into the dogfish's untimely death. The owl disappeared, leaving Bob to break the news to a distraught Beryl.

'What's to become of us, Bob? First the flying school for birds, and now this! How will we feed our kits?'

'I can do it, Beryl. I know I can,' said Bob. 'I can be like a duck. I just need more time.'

'We don't *have* more time, Bob.'

'But, Beryl…'

'Look, Bob, you're just a beaver! Beavers work to get paid, and that's what they're good at. A beaver isn't meant to have his own business, so you'll just have to get on with it!'

Beryl stormed out of the cottage, her head in a spin, to seek comfort from her next door neighbour, Millie. The kindly old beaver put an arm around Beryl's shoulder and took her inside.

'What's the matter, Beryl? Is it the kits? Are they okay?'

'No, it's Bob, and it's all *my* fault. Only for me, he wouldn't have even tried to start his own business. I told him it was all right.'

'You were just being kind, Beryl. It's what Bob wanted.'

'He told me he could do it, Millie. Now we've lost everything.'

'You still have each other, dear.'

'I wish things could be like they were. If only we could just go back to being beavers. I'm so worried, Millie.'

'Hush, Beryl. Things will be fine, you wait and see.'

Back in the cottage, Bob sighed with frustration. Clearly, the flying school was a mistake, and the swimming school had been a complete washout. The truth was that birds remained as much of a mystery to him as ever, and fish even more so. Next time he'd be more careful and check things out in advance. That way, he would know something about the business and not have to rely on the likes of an owl.

Beryl wasn't helping either, thought Bob. To say that he was *just* a beaver simply wasn't fair. Okay, he had hands, but so what? He had a duck's brain, and he could spot opportunities that would be invisible to someone like Beryl. Anyway, who said starting a business would be easy? Sometimes things went wrong, even for ducks. Why couldn't Beryl understand that? It meant you had to try twice as hard the next time, and not just give up like she wanted to do. The most important thing, thought Bob, was to be on the lookout for the next opportunity, and to be ready to grab it when it came along.

21(a) subsection (e) of agreement number F4728Y. I have been instructed by my client to invoke clause 34(c) of the said agreement, unless you comply fully with clause 21(a) subsection (e) within 7 days.

Yours sincerely,
A.J. Fox
Legal Adviser

Although Bob couldn't fully make sense of the words, he knew it must have something to do with the River Bank. He read the parchment a second time and then, tearing off a strip, he stuffed it into his pipe and stared vacantly as it burned slowly, the purple flame providing a semblance of heat. Nine days later a second parchment arrived, and once again Bob stumbled through the words.

13th April
Dear Sir,

I refer to mine of the 4th instance. Pursuant to your failure, as party of the first part, to comply with clause 21(a) subsection (e) of agreement number F4728Y, my client, the River Bank, has hereby instructed me to issue you with notice to quit. Such notice shall take immediate effect under section 12, subsection Q, of the Defaulters' Eviction Act.

Yours sincerely,
A.J. Fox
Legal Adviser

Bob's hands shook as he read it a second time, and though the words seemed to move about on the parchment, the message didn't change. Their home was now the property of the River Bank. The loans had brought nothing but bad luck, thought Bob, his business failures making him the subject of ridicule – and now this. Cursing himself for having borrowed in the first place, Bob stared into space and wondered what to do. It could be a bluff, he thought. Maybe the rat was using the eviction notice to bully him into making repayments. If he was serious, there would be trouble, as they would barricade themselves inside the cottage and refuse to be driven out. Deciding to do nothing for the time being, Bob rolled up the parchment and, standing on tiptoe, he concealed it well out reach.

Edgar the Eagle sat stooped over the desk in his office, reading the eviction order line by line. Everything was in order, as he had feared, and he put the papers to one side and prepared to go out. A visit to the legal fox proved to be a waste of time, and an hour later he was on his way to the River Bank. He arrived as the rat was taking a deposit from a squirrel.

'I'm here about the beaver called Bob,' said Edgar, his comment bringing no response from the rat.

'Here's your receipt,' said the rat, handing a piece of paper to the squirrel.

'If you evict Bob, his family will have nowhere to go,' continued Edgar.

'He should have thought of that sooner,' replied the rat, loading the squirrel's deposit onto a trailer.

'Can't you at least give him a chance to find work?'

'Time is money,' replied the rat, starting to drag the trailer along the tree trunk with his tail.

'Just one month,' pleaded Edgar. 'He'll be able to pay you back then.'

'I've got a business to run,' said the rat, muttering to himself as he disappeared into the vault.

Black Thursday arrived early in Great Eagle Wood, and rubbing the sleep from his eyes, Bob wondered who could be knocking at such an hour.

'I'm coming, I'm coming,' he shouted, throwing his dressing gown on his shoulders before lifting the latch on the front door.

'Are you the personage entitled the beaver called Robert?' asked a senior-looking legal fox, flanked by the goat sheriff and four members of the goat police.

'What?'

'Am I not addressing the said person?' repeated the fox, waving a yellowish parchment in the air.

'That's him all right. He's the beaver who wanted to be his own boss,' said the goat sheriff. Unfurling the parchment, the fox pressed a monocle against his eye and began to read aloud.

'In accordance with section 74 (c) of the tenancy agreement, duly signed with The River Bank, I, A.J. Fox, do inform you that, as the party of the first part to the said agreement, you, the beaver called Robert, are hereby served with notice to quit. This notice shall have immediate effect.'

Removing his monocle, the fox handed the parchment to the goat sheriff as Beryl appeared at the doorway.

'What's going on, Bob? What are the police doing here? Has somebody been hurt?'

Bob shook his head and moved aside as the goat sheriff entered the hallway.

'You'll have to go, Bob,' said one of the goat police, touching him gently on the shoulder.

A large group of beavers had begun to gather, as Bob and a shell-shocked Beryl started to move their family's belongings onto the roadway. Half an hour later they had shifted what they could, and there was a gasp as the goat sheriff snapped a padlock on their door. An elderly beaver stepped forward to protest, and the mood grew ugly when he was pushed away roughly.

'Scum,' screamed a voice as the crowd surged forward, and a stone flew past, grazing one of the goat police, before smashing against the house.

'Let's drive them out,' screamed another beaver, lunging at one of the goat police, who stood his ground and shouted for help. Behind them, the legal fox looked on in terror as angry beavers dragged the goat police to the ground and began to beat them with their fists. The sheriff blew on his emergency whistle, which was then wrestled from his mouth, leaving the eviction team at the mercy of the crowd.

'Finish them off,' urged an elderly beaver, waving his walking stick angrily in the air.

'Stop!' thundered a voice, and a huge beaver forced his way through the crowd and began to free the goat sheriff from his assailants.

'It's Hord,' someone shouted, as the giant beaver helped the sheriff to his feet. Hord, a war veteran who had driven countless armies of invaders from Chestnut Hill, sported a foot-long scar stretching from the underside of his nose to the middle of his chest. On one side of his face a half-ear pointed towards the sky, while on the other its partner was swollen into a horrible outsize shape.

'This is the rat's doing,' bellowed Hord. 'If it wasn't for him, none of this would have happened. I say we march on the River Bank.'

There was a rousing cheer in the clearing as 800 beavers roared their approval. Following their leader's instructions, they armed themselves with sticks and were soon lined up in battle formation, ready to move out.

'Left right, left right…' barked Hord as the beavers began to pound along the path towards the top of Chestnut Hill.

'Where with the River Bank?' roared Hord, thumping the branch of a blackthorn tree off the ground in rhythm with his words.

'Down with the River Bank, down with the River Bank,' came the reply from behind, the beavers beating their sticks off the ground in harmony with their leader.

'Where with the River Bank?' repeated Hord, his thunder increased by the cone-shaped leaf that he held pressed against his mouth.

'Down with the River Bank, down with the River Bank…' chanted the beavers.

'Who did they rob?' demanded Hord.

'The beaver called Bob, the beaver called Bob…' they screamed.

'I said, who did they rob?'

'The beaver called Bob, the beaver called Bob…'

'What will we do?'

'We'll tear him in two, we'll tear him in two…'

They reached the top of Chestnut Hill, and Hord let out a mighty roar as they began their descent towards the River Bank. Behind him the trees shook as 800 beavers roared as one, their voices bringing alarmed animals to their doors.

'Where are you going?' enquired some squirrel youngsters from the safety of their tree house, their question lost amid the stamping feet of the marchers.

'Where with the River Bank?' thundered Hord, the veins bulging in his neck as he turned his head for the response.

'Down with the River Bank, down with the River Bank…'

‘What about the rat?’ bellowed Hord, spitting the words through his teeth.

‘We’ll feed him to the cat, we’ll feed him to the cat…’ was the response, as they came within shouting distance of the River Bank.

‘Beaver cheater!’ roared Hord, and the chant was taken up by his incensed followers, who repeated it over and over.

‘Beaver cheater, beaver cheater…’

At the River Bank, fully aware of the mob’s intent, the rat was daubing a heavy coating of grease on the tree trunk that led to his vault. A team of goat security guards was in place too, but judging by their unease it seemed unlikely they would hold their positions. Despite the gravity of the situation, the rat looked unconcerned.

Two hundred yards away, Hord had the River Bank in his sights, the proximity of the rat’s stronghold increasing his rage even more.

‘Where with the River Bank?’ he screamed, froth and spittle spouting from both sides of his mouth.

‘Down with the River Bank, down with the River Bank…’ came the reply once more, the commotion driving a terrified rabbit to burrow his way underground. Close by, an otter stood his ground, his whiskers twitching as he considered the furious mob that was heading his way. Upon reaching the River Bank, Hord ordered the march to stop and barked out a series of demands about the beaver called Bob. There was no sign of movement from the vault and, led by Hord, the beavers began to chant once again.

‘What about the rat?’

'We'll feed him to the cat, we'll feed him to the cat...'

Suddenly the chanting stopped as the rat emerged from the vault and stood on the far end of the tree trunk.

'What do you want?' he asked, staring defiantly at Hord.

'We're here because of the beaver called Bob.'

'Who?'

'You know who!'

'Go away,' said the rat dismissively, and turning on the tree trunk he scuttled inside the vault and dropped a metal shutter over the entrance. Seeing him disappear, Hord let out a mighty roar and rushed onto the tree trunk, followed by the youngest and most athletic of the beavers. There was a splash as the entire charge slithered on the rat's greasy trap and flew into the water. They re-appeared, a moment later, coughing and spluttering as they surfaced. Hord reached the shore, shook his coat, then re-mounted the pole, only to fall off for a second time.

From a distance, Edgar the Eagle could see nothing amiss as he flew towards the River Bank. Drawing closer, however, he heard Hord roar as he charged the pole for a third time. Edgar swooped alongside and blocked his path.

'We're here for the beaver called Bob,' thundered Hord angrily.

'So am I,' replied Edgar.

'Out of our way, then, and let us get on with it.'

'Storming the River Bank isn't going to help.'

'The rat evicted Bob from his house. Now he's going to pay.'

'Killing the rat will make things worse. Only for him, a

lot of beavers wouldn't have a home,' said Edgar.

'We have no choice,' replied Hord.

'Look, this is a bad time for the beaver called Bob. He lost his home trying to become like a duck. Blame the rat if you like. He could have given Bob more time to pay. Or the goat sheriff could have held back a bit. Maybe it was my fault for signing the eviction order.'

Edgar's admission brought gasps of astonishment from the crowd.

'*You* signed Bob's eviction order?' said Hord.

'The law protects us all, even the rat. Sometimes it works against us, but without it things would be even worse.'

'Worse than being thrown out of your home?'

Edgar looked deep into Hord's eyes, which, though tough and uncompromising, were not hard and unfeeling like those of the rat. Seeing the angry faces of the crowd, Edgar was filled with admiration that so many had marched to help a friend in distress. At that moment Edgar knew that he had found the solution, and he began to address the crowd.

'You, the beavers of Great Eagle Wood, are the worthy descendants of Grom. For generations you have worked and toiled to make this wood what it is. It is because of you that the animals of this great wood prosper and live together in peace. Do you want to destroy all that you and your ancestors have helped to create? You can demolish the River Bank and put the rat to the sword. But what will it accomplish? The next time a beaver needs a loan, who will he turn to?'

'Are you saying we should turn a blind eye and let Bob be thrown out of his house?' demanded Hord.

'You're right. The descendants of Grom cannot stand idly by and allow Bob to be driven from his home. But what if there was another way?'

'Another way?' spat Hord impatiently. 'What do you mean *another way*?'

'Is there anyone among you who hasn't hit on hard times?'

The beavers looked at one another and shrugged their shoulders as Edgar continued.

'Would any of you lend Bob a little of what you have yourself?'

There was silence for a moment as the beavers looked at one another again, and began to whisper in little groups.

'I'd lend to Bob,' said an out-of-breath elderly beaver, who had only just caught up with the march.

'So would I,' said a second.

'I'd help Bob,' said several others, and soon there was agreement in all sections of the crowd, as the beavers broke into a rousing chant.

'We'll help Bob, we'll help Bob…'

Edgar opened his wings to quell the noise, but it was some minutes before he could continue.

'This day, my friends, the beavers of Great Eagle Wood, such worthy descendants of Grom, have made a stand for the lofty principles you hold so dear. Your belief in justice will open every padlock, and tonight Bob and his family will sleep peacefully in their beds. From this day onward, beavers will save for beavers, and beavers will lend to beavers. A great institution will be formed, which will come to be known as 'Savings and Loan', and because of it, no beaver in Great Eagle Wood need ever be homeless again.'

Turning towards the vault, Edgar called to the rat, who lifted the metal shutter.

'What do you want?'

'Will you tell the sheriff to open the padlock on Bob's house?'

'Why should I?' asked the rat, staring defiantly at Edgar and the beavers who were gathered on the riverbank.

'Because Bob can pay back his loan.'

'With what?'

'With the money his friends are lending him,' replied Edgar.

'What friends?'

'The beavers.'

'The beavers! That's a joke,' said the rat, his tone almost goading Hord into charging the pole for a fourth time.

'I'll guarantee it,' said Edgar.

'Very well. It's your loss,' replied the rat indifferently.

With that, he disappeared into the vault, and the beavers on the River Bank began to whisper amongst themselves, the younger ones still hoping that peace might be averted. Edgar thanked them once again, and then at a signal from Hord they began to disperse.

That afternoon the sheriff removed the padlock, allowing Beryl to return to her cottage. Bob spent the evening thanking their friends, greeting well-wishers and feeling good to be a beaver. He arrived home to find Beryl weeping in the kitchen.

'What is it? What's wrong?' he asked her.

'Where were you, Bob? The kits cried themselves to sleep.'

'I'm sorry, Beryl, I was just…'

'Imagine, Bob! Having to beg for help. I'm so ashamed.'

'But they're our friends.'

'I'll never be able to face them again!'

'We'll pay them back, love. Wait and see.'

'Pay them back with what, Bob? With words?'

'You're just upset, Beryl. Wait until tomorrow.'

'Tomorrow? There won't *be* any tomorrow!'

'Don't say that, love. I know you're angry, but…'

'You'll have to choose, Bob,' said Beryl, her voice firm.

'What do you mean, choose?'

'Starting your own business has brought us nothing except misery.'

'Listen, Beryl, please…'

'You listen to me, Bob! I've been a beaver all my life. All I want is to be able to pay the bills and have enough for food. But that's not good enough for you. You want to be your own boss and live in a fancy house. It's just a dream, Bob, and it's turning into a nightmare!'

'I don't want it for myself, Beryl. It's for you and the kits. I…'

'If you want to be like a duck, you'd better leave! It's either them or us, Bob. So make up your mind.'

'But, Beryl…'

Bob sat staring into the darkness as Beryl covered her head and cried bitterly. Knowing that it was beyond him, he didn't try to comfort her. Her words had hurt him, and at that moment, even if she needed him, he could not have gone to her. Instead, he sat there and cursed himself for wanting to be like a duck. Now Beryl was forcing him to choose. Them or us, she had said, meaning leave or stay. It was his decision, and he would have to make up his mind.

Chapter Five

The following day began like any other on the River Bank. Rising at seven, the rat took a lighted candle from its holder and checked for signs of a break-in during the night. He began at the entrance, a door of solid timber that the rat considered to be practically impenetrable. A narrow corridor, cut from the insides of a fallen oak, stretched southwards from the entrance, with small rooms to either side providing office and living space. At the far end, guarded by a heavy-set double door, was the vault, which housed gold and silver coins of various denominations. An area of dense thorny undergrowth lay beyond, making access from the rear an impossibility.

Satisfied that all was in order, the rat retraced his steps towards the kitchen, where a shimmer of half-light had begun to filter through a crack in the ceiling. Cleaning dust embers from the grate, he set a fresh log fire, and washed himself with water that had been warming beside the fireplace. A breakfast of bread and cheese was washed down with warm milk, and he was ready for work.

Leaving the kitchen, the rat moved briskly towards the vault, where he quickly located a concealed pulley. He tugged repeatedly on the rope, the strain showing on his face as the door creaked slowly open. Inside, a candle-lit chamber contained tiered rows of coins, stacked according to value. There were three rows of silver on the bottom, and the rat entered the total of each into a large hard-back ledger. The two rows at the top contained gold coins, which he counted even more meticulously and recorded in a separate column of the ledger.

Turning the pages, the rat surveyed the previous month's records, which showed the same painstaking attention to detail. Further back were his father's entries, and his grandfather's further back still. The rat paused for a moment, knowing that when the time was right, one of *his* sons would take over the mantle and ensure that the age-old traditions of the River Bank would continue. Already one of his offspring was displaying the type of acumen the business demanded. Attention to detail was a prerequisite, and any rat found wanting in this regard was unsuitable at source. Good judgement was essential too, as one bad debt required a multitude of good ones to recover the loss. Refraining from friendship came next – it was a commodity that no rat could value highly. Sensible banking left no room for sentiment, which was an expensive luxury likely to cloud one's judgement. Business was business, and a proposition either stood up to scrutiny or it didn't. A lesser rat, influenced by feelings, wouldn't have called time on the beaver called Bob, choosing instead to relent in the face of intimidation and the special pleadings of Edgar the Eagle.

Opening the ledger on the page that contained the last of his father's entries, the rat almost felt a tinge of emotion as he remembered his own succession to high office. Sensing that his time was short, from his deathbed his father had looked at each of his sons, before beckoning *him* to come forward. 'A borrower and a lender be,' he had whispered in his ear, and with the weight of responsibility lifted, he expired almost as soon as the baton was passed.

At nine o'clock the rat opened the door of the bank and stood for a moment to sniff the morning air. He shivered a little as an icy gust of wind tested the hairs on his back, unmasking a vulnerability that was exploited by a nearby bullfrog.

'Cold, huh?'

The rat stared at him indifferently and said nothing.

'Any chance of a loan?'

'He'll pay you back,' said a second frog. 'Even cut you into his profits.'

'You'll be rich!' promised the bullfrog. 'You can put your feet up.'

Ignoring the growing array of enticements, the rat readied his trailer and scuttled along the oak towards a group of beavers queuing on the River Bank. Drawing closer, he was surprised by their freshness of face. Normally the younger beavers arrived at closing time, red-faced and out of breath, to lodge whatever they had managed to put aside. Saving was what beavers did best, thought the rat – unlike ducks, they lacked the creativity needed to invest money more productively.

'Lodgements?' asked the rat expectantly, unhitching the trailer as he arrived at the River Bank.

'We're withdrawing cash for the beaver called Bob,' replied the youngest.

Edgar added milk and stirred in some sugar. Then, sitting back in his chair, he sipped the tea and watched the rat squirm and sweat. How many times, he wondered, had he presided with indifference as hard-pressed animals pleaded for more money or more time? How many animals had been left without hope as he lined his pockets at their expense? Now it was his turn to feel the heat, and though he might have been reluctant to admit it, Edgar was enjoying himself.

'Let me get one thing straight, rat,' he asked, sitting forward in his chair. 'Are you saying that your bank doesn't *have* the beavers' money?'

'Of course I have their money,' snapped the rat, finding it increasingly hard to control his temper.

'So what's the problem then?'

'The problem is that I don't have their money in the *vault*.'

'You don't? But I thought you said …'

'The ducks have their money, and the squirrels and the goats, and everyone else who took out loans. You even have some of it yourself.'

'I have?' said Edgar, feigning surprise.

Faced with Edgar's indifference, the strain was showing on the rat's face as he leaned forward in his chair.

'Why don't you explain that to the beavers?' asked Edgar, smiling. 'Tell them they'll have to wait to get their money back. You can always say that the ducks have it.'

'It's no laughing matter,' said the rat crossly. 'If you hadn't intervened for the beaver called Bob, none of this would have happened in the first place.'

Edgar shrugged his shoulders, and the rat rose to leave, firing a final parting shot as he disappeared through the door.

'I'm holding *you* responsible for this, Edgar. If my bank goes under, I'll take you with me.'

Back at the River Bank, the queue was growing and the rat feared the worst as he re-opened for the afternoon. By three o'clock he was down to the last row of coins, and there was still an hour to go before the ducks would arrive with their lodgements. At half past three he filled the trailer with the last of the gold, and collected yet another list of withdrawal requests. He returned to the vault, where a search yielded only a handful of mixed coins that had fallen behind the bottom row of timber. Reaching blindly into hidden nooks and crannies, the rat's efforts echoed around the empty chamber, but he failed to add to what had already been found.

This is it, he thought, looking at the picture of his father that hung in the corridor outside the vault. Would *he* have foreseen the consequences of evicting the beaver called Bob? Would he have given out less in loans and held more cash in the vault? He remembered how a run on the bank had been his father's greatest nightmare and how he had watched constantly for the spark that would ignite it. Fortunately, it had never come to pass in his lifetime.

The rat removed the portraits of his ancestors from the walls to protect them from the shame that was unfolding before their eyes. Issuing instructions to the swans, he hitched up the empty trailer, covered it with a cloth and began what would almost certainly be his last journey across the oak. In the distance, the old beavers waited calmly, oblivious to the rat's plight. They would listen open-mouthed, he thought, as he explained how there was a 'temporary shortage of funds'.

Then, once they realised that he didn't have their money, the real trouble would start. Fortunately, age would prevent them from giving chase, but that would merely prolong his agony; the younger beavers, on hearing what had happened, would hunt him down relentlessly.

On the River Bank, the beavers watched as the rat pulled what appeared to be another load of gold across the oak. Any second now he would unveil a trailer full of nothing, and the beavers' eyes would open wide in disbelief. Then, when he had almost reached the River Bank, it happened. Having greased the oak to derail Hord and his invading beavers the previous day, during the morning's withdrawals the rat had successfully negotiated the sneaky trap. This time, however, losing his balance, he toppled sideways from the pole and hit the water with the trailer in hot pursuit. The old beavers watched in amazement as the rat disappeared from view. A moment later he resurfaced, making frantic efforts to stop himself being pulled under for a second time. Eventually, managing to detach himself from the trailer, he hauled himself onto the oak and collapsed with exhaustion.

Five minutes later the episode was repeated, the rat again slipping on the oak and dumping another trailer-load of 'gold' into the river. This time the beavers were not amused.

'He doesn't want to give us our money,' cried one, waving his walking stick in the air.

'Maybe he doesn't have our money,' suggested a second beaver, as the rat emerged from the depths, feigning innocence of whatever wrongdoing he was accused.

'The rat's taking us for fools,' barked another. 'He's falling in on purpose.'

It was 3.50 pm, and the rat was counting down the time. In ten minutes the ducks would arrive, laden with cash, and his problems would be solved. On the River Bank, however, tempers were rising as the beavers grew tired of waiting. Suddenly, there was a flurry of movement in the water, and the single voice swans began to attack each other viciously. Moving their necks from side to side, they thrust their heads forward, like one-handed boxers searching for an opening. Feathers flew into the air as the swans spat at each other and fought fiercely. Forgetting their problems, the beavers began to place bets with money that the rat didn't have.

'Go on, hit him, stop dancing around,' shouted a grandfather beaver, leaning so far forward that he almost toppled into the water.

'Ouch!' said another, as the smaller swan took a blow to his head.

At 3.59 the fight ended as abruptly as it had begun, the larger swan turning his back as his companion gave chase.

'Coward, you're twice the size of him!' screamed a losing punter, as the smaller swan's backers celebrated their good fortune.

At 4.01, from inside the vault, the rat scanned the crowd at the River Bank. Where were the ducks, he wondered. They should have arrived by now, or at least be visible in the distance, weighed down with their money bags bursting to the brim. By 4.05 the rat was starting to panic, knowing that unless the ducks arrived soon the swans' impressive brawl would have been a waste of time. Then, spotting an unmistakeable swagger, he punched the air as the duck called Bill joined the end of the queue. Now it was just a matter of getting him into the bank, something that would have to be done without arousing the suspicion of the beavers.

A moment later there was a chorus of boos from the beavers as the swans swam past again, this time leaning amorously towards each other.

'It's a fix! I knew it all along,' shouted a beaver, throwing a stone that landed short of its target.

'Sissies,' shouted another, and abandoning his crutch, he put his fingers in his mouth to whistle rudely.

Ignoring the barracking, the swans floated gracefully past. Moving together as one, they rounded a bend in the river and disappeared from view. A minute later they were docking beside the vault, where the rat lay in wait.

'Nice one,' said the duck called Bill, who had spent the crossing wedged securely between the swans. Leaning first to one side and then the other, he slipped a sack of money from his back.

'Great idea, rat, to send out those swans. I thought I'd never get outta that queue. What's with those beavers? The way they're carryin' on, you'd think the bank was runnin' outta money!'

'That's beavers for you,' said the rat, wiping beads of perspiration from his forehead. 'Anyway, I'm glad to be of help, Bill. After all, a busy duck like you can't be waiting around in beaver queues. Come on in, and we'll have tea while we sort out your lodgement.'

That night, over on the east of the wood, a mother kissed her little eagle gently on the forehead.

'Sweet dreams, Abby.'

'But, Mum, it's still bright outside.'

'You've got a busy day tomorrow, darling. It's best to have your beauty sleep.'

'But Granddad said he'd tell me a story. He promised.'

'Your granddad is a busy eagle, Abby. Maybe he'll come tomorrow night.'

Abby closed her eyes and waited for her mother to leave the room. She listened to the footsteps dying away before throwing back her covers and peering through a gap in the curtain. Outside, some squirrels were playing on the branches of an oak tree and, standing on tiptoe, Abby stretched to follow their movements. Suddenly, they stopped and pointed in her direction.

'Abby's in bed! Abby's in bed! Na na, na na na!'

Jumping away from the window, Abby flung herself angrily onto the bed. It wasn't fair, the squirrels got to stay up as late as they liked, she thought, burying her face in the pillow. It was nearly dark when she ventured back to the curtain and, looking skywards, she searched for her granddad in the half-light. Returning to her bed, the little eagle's eyes grew heavy and she was almost asleep when she was startled by a knock on the window.

'Granddad! You came. You're the best in the world.'

'Of course I came,' said Edgar, smiling as his granddaughter hugged him excitedly.

'Promises are for keeping, Abby, especially important ones like telling a goodnight story.'

'Will you tell me about Great Eagle Wood, Granddad?'

'I don't know. It's getting late. Your mother will be...'

'You promised! Pleeease? I'll be ever so good.'

The little eagle begged and begged, and Edgar felt his resistance melt as he perched himself at the side of her bed.

'Well, things were different when I was your age, Abby. There was no electricity then. All we had was the light from the sun.'

'What about candles, Granddad?'

'Yes, there were some, but not everyone could afford them.'

'Were there glow-worms?'

'Ah yes. Every house had a welcome for glow-worms. My mother relied on them to get her knitting done.'

'Did you have fires, Granddad?'

'Yes, fires were our only means of heat. During the day we'd collect sticks, and in the evenings my father would stack them in the fireplace and set them alight. Then we'd curl up and listen to the stories.'

'Stories? What kind of stories?'

'About the Great Eagle and how he created the wood. Sometimes, the old-timers used to talk about the Dians.'

'The Dians?'

'They were the tribes who used to live in the wood, Abby. Some say they were badly treated, but that one's for another day.'

'Did the old-timers tell *scary* stories?'

'I remember one goat who had a long white beard. He used to sit by the fire and fill his pipe. Then he'd light it up and keep puffing until the room was full of smoke. After that he'd start with his stories, scary ones about headless horses and geese with mad eyes. When he finished, we'd go to bed with the sheets over our heads.'

'Wow!'

'No one tells stories now, Abby.'

'Not even about eagles?'

'My father used to tell of a time when eagles could talk to the wind and the sky.'

'Really?'

'Then we lost interest, he said.'

'In talking to the wind and the sky?'

'That's right, and now we can't do it anymore.'

'Is *everything* different, Granddad? To the way it used to be.'

'Not everything, Abby. Your mother's as good a cook as there's ever been.'

'Yeah, but what about other things?'

'The biggest change is the amount of choice nowadays. Take banks – in my day we only had one.'

'Was that the River Bank?'

'Aren't you the clever eagle! I remember how every Thursday my mother would count whatever she had managed to save. On Friday, my father used to lodge it at the River Bank. Sometimes, if there was a special occasion, he might take out a loan. Like the time Uncle Tom came to visit…'

After a while, Abby's eyes began to flicker and, though she battled to keep them open, before long the little eagle was asleep. Beside her, perched on a chair, Edgar was drifting too, breathing deeply, his head resting on his chest. In his dream he was young again, and his face softened into a smile as he drifted back to a time long ago.

Chapter Six

What began as a routine eviction had brought the rat to the point of bankruptcy and he spent the weekend reflecting on his ordeal. First, Hord and his murdering beavers had taken the law into their own hands. Then, only the last minute arrival of the duck called Bill had saved him from certain ruin. No doubt the beavers would have hunted him down like a criminal, and he would now be in hiding. Worse still, he might already have fallen into their hands, begging to be put to death as they tortured him mercilessly.

A strange way of showing their gratitude, the rat thought, after all he had done for them. Almost every beaver with a roof over his head had him to thank for it. Still, knowing them as well as he did, he should have expected as much. Beavers were a thankless lot, taking what they could and giving nothing in return. Edgar, however, should have known better. It was he who had incited the beavers to demand their money, and when the rat made a lunchtime plea for help,

Edgar had scoffed at his plight. It would be different in future, thought the rat. Next time, he'd make sure there was enough in the vault to survive any onslaught. He would lend less and charge higher rates of interest. That way he'd have more money in the vault, and still earn just as much.

Now that the newly established Savings and Loan Association was catering for their borrowing needs, the cutbacks at the River Bank had little impact on the beavers. Ironically, it was the ducks who, having saved the rat from ruin, were hardest hit. In May an ambitious duck had started to build a railroad across the Great Wood, but was stopped in his tracks when the rat refused him a loan. In the same month another duck was forced to shelve plans for a new system of gas lighting. Even the duck called Bill was a victim of the credit squeeze, as the rat rejected a loan application to extend his pillow shop. It was obvious that the economy in the wood was slowing down, a fact made clear by the sign in the window of a greengrocer shop: 'Tomato plants for sale – while stalks last'. At a meeting with Edgar the Eagle, the ducks complained bitterly.

'That rat's stone crazy,' said the railroad duck. 'He wouldn't give ya money for nothin'.'

'He's gone outta his head,' said the duck called Bill. 'Why, I had the Beaver Construction Team lined up to start work on my extension. Then the rat turns me down like I was gettin' the money for free. I'm tellin' ya, that rat's suffered a change o' personality. He must 'ave got hit on the head by a tree or somethin'. The way he's carryin' on, we'll all be outta business.'

Edgar nodded and agreed that they would have to come

up with a plan. The trouble was, what plan? He could talk to the rat, but he doubted if it would do much good. After all, the rat blamed *him* for almost running out of money. Back in his office, he wondered what could be done. If the rat wouldn't finance the ducks, who would? They could borrow from one another, of course, like the beavers were doing. The trouble was that the ducks put everything they had back into their business. So, as they had no savings, they had nothing to lend.

Later that evening the sun was drifting lower in the sky as Edgar paced up and down in his office. It had almost disappeared behind the treetops when a sudden thought made him stop. Then, starting to walk up and down again, he tossed the idea around in his head. Would it work, he wondered. If the ducks agreed to it, there was a good chance that it would.

There was only one way to find out. Leaving his office, Edgar headed straight for the duck called Bill's house. On arrival, he was subjected to the same rant that he had listened to earlier.

'I'm tellin' ya, Mr Edgar, that rodent's goin' to be the death o' me. For years I've been buildin' up my business, an' now the rat treats me like a good for nothin'. How am I goin' to expand without capital? You tell me, Mr Edgar, or I'm a dead duck.'

Edgar stared at the duck called Bill, and wondered if he was ready for the proposition that was about to come his way. Ducks were smart, and generally they had an open mind, but there was always a danger of trying to push them too far. Edgar took a deep breath.

'Would you be willing to sell part of your pillow business, Bill?'

Edgar's intake of breath seemed shallow compared to the gust inhaled by the duck called Bill. He tried to speak, but could squeeze nothing out.

'You'd have money to expand your business, without having to borrow from the rat,' continued Edgar.

Mention of the rat jogged Bill from near unconsciousness. His eyes misted over, and he looked as though he was about to cry.

'Are ya askin' me to sell my pillow business, Mr Edgar?'

'Not *all* of your business. Just enough to help you expand your shop. You'd still be the boss, of course.'

'I see.'

'Most folk out there don't have your brains, Bill, but they'd jump at the chance of buying into pillows. Call them sleeping partners if you like.'

'Sleepin' partners! So now I've got guys tellin' me how to sell pillows. Like the partner my cousin Norman took on. That fella didn't have the brains of a rockin' horse.'

'It's not like that, Bill. Folk would just pay their money and sit back. You'd still be running the business.'

'I dunno. It all sounds a bit strange to me, Mr Edgar.'

'Look, I have to get back to the office. Why don't you think it over?'

After Edgar had left, Bill thought about nothing else. His love affair with pillows had begun the day he was born, and he remembered their first kiss as if it were yesterday. Hesitating at first, he moved closer as the pillow's soft downy scent drew him in. Then, nestling alongside, he closed his eyes and felt his skin tingle as his puckered lips made contact. Afterwards, not wanting to let go, he had lain there, staring at the ceiling, until his mother's voice tore him from heaven.

'Let that pillow alone, ya stupid duck. You'll have those feathers worn out with yer carry on.'

Childhood games allowed Bill to apply the social skills he was born with, and school taught him what little nature had left out. Throughout it all, pillows remained his first love, and it was no surprise when he began to sell them, doing for pleasure what other folk called work.

Selling his business was a prospect Bill had not even remotely considered. It would, he thought, be like cutting off one of his hands – if he had hands. So the answer was *no*, and if the rat wouldn't lend him money to expand, he would just hold on to what he had. That night, Bill snuggled up to his pillows and slept like a duckling, blissfully unaware of how an encounter with a stranger was about to change everything.

The following day, he set off early to tell Edgar of his decision not to sell. He had gone almost halfway when, a short distance ahead, something stepped from the undergrowth onto the path.

'Howdy, stranger,' said a green-headed duck called a mallard, who was smiling as he approached.

'Hi,' said Bill, his eyes drawn to a copper container that the mallard was making no effort to conceal.

'Sleep will be history once guys get a hold o' this stuff,' said the mallard, nodding towards the rather unpleasant-smelling liquid in the container.

'Huh?'

'One sniff o' this stuff, and you'll be awake for days. An' nights too,' laughed the mallard. 'Who'll want pillows then?'

'Are ya sayin' that pillows are goin' outta fashion?'

'Obsoletely!' said the mallard.

'What am I goin' to do?' asked the duck, his face starting to turn pale. 'Pillows are my business.'

'If I was you I'd stop makin' 'em right now,' advised the mallard. 'Maybe sell off what ya have in stock. It'll take a couple o' weeks for this potion to catch on.'

'Ya mean I'm goin' to have to stop makin' pillows?'

'Nothin' lasts forever,' said the mallard, shrugging his shoulders.

Accepting an invitation to see the potion in action, Bill returned to the mallard's house with him. They played games of chess to pass the time, and regular cups of tea helped Bill to stay sharp.

'Checkmate!'

The mallard's green head shook as he conceded, bringing the score to six nil. He was under pressure again in game seven as Bill, despite playing with the black pieces, capitalised on his superior intelligence.

'Checkmate! That's seven nil to me.'

The mallard nodded and clenched his mouth to stifle a yawn. Excusing himself from the table, he withdrew to an adjoining room.

'I'm just takin' a top-up of this miracle potion, buddy. Be back in a jiffy.'

A moment later he reappeared, looking fresher than before and even a fraction taller. Seeing Bill stare at a spot on his chin, he blinked self-consciously.

buy into pillows your money will be growin' so fast you won't have time to count it.'

Edgar's choice was an inspired one, and Bill sold off a quarter share of his business in less than a day. When other ducks learned of Bill's success, some decided to take their businesses public too. The bull was always positive about new stocks.

'Anythin' that lies between the ground and the sky is worth buyin' in this wood. Why, there's even value to be got underground if ya ask me.'

Pretty soon, stocks were selling in every type of business, and prices just kept on rising.

Amid the euphoria, Edgar became concerned that things were moving too fast. Given their rate of increase, it was clear that sooner or later stock prices would tumble and send the fledgling market into freefall. Another problem was the bull, who was exploiting his position as the wood's sole investment adviser.

'I'll tell ya, I've never met anyone who can charge like that bull,' said the duck called Bill, who was making so much money himself, that he was unconcerned about the bull's excesses.

It mattered to Edgar on both fronts. Pushing prices too high could be damaging in the long term, and overcharging by the bull had to be stamped out immediately. Also, a shortage of ducks wishing to sell stocks meant that those wanting to buy were often left disappointed. Fortunately, Edgar had a solution for all three problems, and he knew immediately who could provide it.

The brown bear had seen portents of doom for as long as anyone could remember. Longer nights and lower skies meant that the end of time wasn't far off, he claimed, his forecasts being so vague as to be difficult to refute. Turning good news into bad, the bear's negativity left him in a dark mood that rarely lifted. His views were widely feared in Great Eagle Wood, and the bear's sell recommendations soon had stock prices falling to well below their highs.

'Pillows? I don't see much of a future for pillows,' said the brown bear. 'Why, there's even talk that some mallard's got a potion that will do away with sleep. Pillows are a waste of money if you ask me.'

Soon, the weekly stock market came to be one of the best attended events in the wood. Situated at the end of a well-located street, a high wall provided shelter for the buyers, who began to assemble from early morning. There, the farm bull entered their orders in a ledger, writing their offer price in the centre column and adding his commission in the margin. On the other side of the wall were the sellers, many of whom were ducks hoping to raise money to expand their businesses. Alongside them, other animals, believing that stock prices were about to fall, were selling too. Growling loudly, the brown bear took their instructions, which he recorded in his 'sell book'.

Every so often a bell rang, and this was a signal for the farm bull and the brown bear to match buyers and sellers. Sometimes there were more buyers, and a bull market saw prices rise on the back of the farm bull's infectious optimism. Other times, a bear market dragged prices down, as the brown bear's gloomy predictions brought sellers out in force.

Meanwhile, Edgar the Eagle sat back and watched the Great Wood grow and prosper like never before. Everywhere, ducks were busy with new inventions, which beavers and other animals had an opportunity to invest in. Strange machines, which could cut grass and wash dishes, began to appear, and the tap-tapping of typewriters could be heard throughout the wood. Edgar's favourite invention was the telephone, which would soon become the talk of the wood. There were larger projects too, like the network of giant railways that began to stretch north to south, and from east to west across Great Eagle Wood.

In times of transition, there are always those who are left behind, and so it was with Bob's partner, Beryl. It wasn't that she didn't notice change – she most certainly did – but she wasn't really interested in being a part of it. The fact that one day followed another was not a problem, and the change of the seasons was something she was okay with too. Beryl, you see, was comfortable with change that came slowly. That Friday, as she looked in the mirror, she saw something that she had not noticed before. Beryl laughed at first, thinking the line to be an imperfection in the glass. When it remained, despite her efforts with a cloth, she began to wiggle her head from side to side. Still, the line remained, the twisting of her face, if anything, causing it to lengthen a little. It faded when she stepped back, only to return again when curiosity drew her back in.

'It's a wrinkle, Beryl,' said Bob matter-of-factly as he passed on his way to the kitchen. 'You've got a wrinkle on your face.'

Beryl opened her mouth to issue a denial, but the movement made the wrinkle stretch downwards in the direction of her chin. She saw a second one then, its presence obscured by her breath on the glass as she edged closer. She wiped it clear, but saw the fog return once more as her breath quickened. Beryl started to panic; raising both hands, she held her face taut and began searching its contours. Wanting to find nothing, she was aware nonetheless of the urgency of knowing. Working their way downwards, her fingertips negotiated a smooth passage from forehead to eye level. Pausing beside her nose, they regained momentum as the search continued. Then, sucked in by her lips, they slowed again, before finally drawing a line at her chin.

Beryl sighed as she drew her fingers back and forth, the wrinkle on her chin appearing to lengthen as she continued to explore. Were there others, she wondered, quickly moving her hands up and down and to the side. She remembered how the same thing had happened to her mother, her smooth face becoming chiselled with lines almost overnight.

'It's just a wrinkle,' said Bob, putting an arm around her shoulder.

'What do you mean, just a wrinkle?'

'Everyone gets them, Beryl. Even beavers.'

'But I don't want wrinkles! I want to stay the same.'

That night, kept awake by the pounding of her heart, Beryl lay facing the ceiling. She could either stand far enough back from the mirror in future, she thought, or cloud the issue by getting up close. But either way she would still know that she was getting old and wrinkled. If only things could stay just as they were, she thought. Then she would be happy forever.

Two feet away, Bob lay staring into the darkness. That morning, stocks had hit record highs, and he had watched the ducks grow richer, longing to be a part of it. Would things always be the same, he wondered. Was he to be a beaver forever, condemned to take orders, never to be his own boss? Sighing with frustration, Bob dug his head into the pillow and wondered how much longer he could carry on.

And so it was that the two beavers lay, separately, each wanting what the other already had. One, craving the comfort of sameness, balked at change and its unkind face. The other, held back by patterns and routine, dreamt of being like a duck and moving on. Suddenly, from the darkness came light, as a beam from the night sky penetrated the curtains and filled the space between the beavers. A moment later it was gone.

BOTTOM
LINE

Chapter Seven

Pillow stocks were up again, observed Edgar, as he studied the morning's business headlines. It was the third increase in as many weeks, as rumours that a mallard had invented a 'no sleep' potion continued to recede. The duck called Bill would be pleased, he thought, as he poured himself another cup of tea. Adding a spoon of sugar, he was about to stir in a second when he remembered his doctor's warnings.

'Miss Abby is here, sir,' announced a goat guard, opening the door to Edgar's study.

'Show her in, please.'

'Yes, sir.'

Edgar checked the sports news as he waited for his granddaughter to appear. So much time had passed, he thought, since Abby used to beg for a bedtime story. She was finished school now, and her daily skirmishes with squirrel youngsters were a thing of the past. Abby had matured, of that there was no doubt.

'Are you ready, Granddad?' she demanded, bursting into the room. 'Mum says you need a break. She says you've been working too hard.'

Edgar smiled as his granddaughter chided him for his attention to detail. She was so like her mother, he thought – impossible to sidetrack once she got something into her head.

'Let's go to the Freedom Tower, Granddad. Like we said.'

'Of course, Abby. Come on, you lead the way.'

They left the building and Edgar was content to follow in the youngster's slipstream as she soared skywards. Seconds later she was riding the wind expertly, gliding in and out, as air currents threatened to throw her off course.

'Are you okay, Granddad?'

'Sure, I'm right behind you, Abby.'

'Okay, hang on, we're going in.'

Edgar took an extra breath as the descent began. Below him, Abby was swooping downwards, and twenty seconds later they had landed on top of the Freedom Tower.

'Well done,' wheezed Edgar, his chest heaving as his lungs adapted to the suddenness of their arrival.

'Thanks, Granddad.'

'For what?'

'For bringing me here. The Freedom Tower is my favourite place in the whole wood.'

Edgar smiled, knowing that it was really *she* who had brought *him*. Nestling under his wing, Abby gazed into the vastness of the Great Wood.

'Can you feel it, Granddad?'

Edgar felt his skin tingle and the feathers on his back stiffen. He knew that they could leave now, or if they wished they could stay forever. They could soar towards the sun, float with the wind or go gently to ground. They could speak their mind, plan their futures or reflect on things past. Or they could dream, and know that those dreams could come to pass. What the Great Eagle had gifted them had been guarded well, so well that one so young could feel its force.

'Yes, Abby. I can feel it too. Freedom is the most precious gift of all. This tower is a symbol of all that we are. Treasure it as long as you live.'

Abby nodded, her attention distracted by a movement on the ground to the east of the Freedom Tower. Swaggering along the path was a duck with a knapsack strapped neatly on his back. On his chest hung a brightly coloured sign, advertising the nature of his services.

'Look at that, Granddad!'

Edgar struggled to make out the words, his eyes straining with effort as he read out each letter separately.

'S-a-v-e y-o-u-r s-o-l-e'. Ingenious,' he said, admiring the inventiveness of the shoe repair sign.

'He's a door-to-door duck, Abby. Let's see him in action.'

The eagles watched from the Freedom Tower as the duck stopped on the path and took a face-sized mirror from his knapsack. Moving his head from side to side, he gave an admiring whistle before kissing the mirror and returning it to his sack. Holding a tiny polishing brush in his bill, he buffed his shoes until they glinted in the sunlight, then scanned a blue notebook containing a list of potential customers. Deciding on a number, he knocked on a nearby door. It was opened by a gruff-looking badger, who stared impassively as the duck produced his killer opening line.

'Good day, sir. I have come to save your sole.'

'I'm not a believer,' snapped the badger crossly.

'Neither am I,' replied the door-to-door duck, smiling confidently and thrusting a foot as far forward as circumstances would permit. Responding instinctively, the badger wedged a foot of his own in the doorway, blocking any prospect of a further advance by his caller. It was a move that would have played into the duck's hands, if he had hands. Set against his own shiny leather, the badger's tatty uppers looked worn and dull.

'We have a special offer today, sir. Two shoes repaired for the price of one.'

The badger's face softened as he eyed his caller's shiny black shoes against his own pair of faded grey. Seizing the opportunity, the duck pressed home his advantage.

'And I'll throw in a shoe shine for free. Now there's an offer! What do you say, sir?'

From the top of the Freedom Tower the eagles watched the badger step to one side as the duck swaggered confidently past him into the house.

'Aren't ducks smart, Granddad? They have such clever ideas.'

'Nobody is smarter, Abby.'

'Nobody except you, Granddad.'

Edgar smiled, knowing that in a way his granddaughter was right. Ducks were smart, that much everyone knew, but whereas their focus was on their own business, Edgar had to look out for everyone. Seeing the bigger picture was what set eagles apart, and Edgar most of all.

'When I'm older, Granddad…'

'Yes, Abby?'

Edgar waited and wondered what his granddaughter was about to say. Youngsters had changed so much, he thought, and material wealth mattered more than ever before. Did she want to make a million, even if it wasn't what eagles did best? Or would she want to travel and broaden her mind?

'When I grow up, I want to be like you, Granddad.'

Edgar nodded, wondering which of his special traits Abby liked best. He was wise, most animals would agree on that. He was personable and fair too, and good at solving problems. It surprised him that one so young would be perceptive enough to notice.

'So you want to be like me, Abby? In what way, exactly?'

'I want to be a great leader. Just like you, Granddad.'

Edgar took a deep breath, and wondered if such a thing were possible. His granddaughter loved the Great Wood, which in a way was what mattered most of all. She was bright too, and a good listener – an ability that was as important as any other. Yet there *was* a problem. The Great Wood had never elected a female leader, nor had the prospect ever been raised. Would it be right to raise her hopes, and have them crushed by a wood that wasn't ready for change?

'Abby, there's something that you should know,' he began hesitantly.

'Yes, Granddad?'

Edgar looked into his granddaughter's eyes, and knew that she had a right to dream. It was what made the Great Wood great: no goal was unachievable, no barrier so high that it could not be scaled.

'You'll make a fine leader, Abby. Maybe the best the Great Wood has ever seen. If that's your dream, don't ever let it go.'

'Thanks, Granddad. You're my hero.'

'Come on, Abby. I want you to meet one of *my* heroes.'

Travelling swiftly, the two eagles quickly passed over the hill to the east, and soon they had put a densely populated plateau area behind them. From there it was a short flight to the high street and the duck called Bill's shop. To become leader of the Great Wood, there was much that Abby needed to learn, and where better to start, thought Edgar.

'Ah, Mr Edgar, sir. Come in. How nice to see you.'

'Thanks, Bill. I don't know how you do it. Another new shop!'

'Ya can't stand still, Mr Edgar. Either ya grow or ya die. That's what I say!'

'You've achieved so much already, Bill.'

'You gotta have a plan, Mr Edgar. An' once ya achieve it, ya gotta make a new one. Ya can't stand still in this wood, that's for sure. 'Cause if yer not goin' up, next thing yer goin' to be comin' down.'

Edgar nodded in admiration. Staying hungry was what mattered most, he thought, the next customer always providing a new challenge. It was ducks like Bill who made the Great Wood what it was.

'I've brought my granddaughter along with me today, Bill. This is Abby.'

'Come right on in, Miss Abby, an' make yerself at home.'

'I'm pleased to meet you, Mr Bill.'

'The pleasure's all mine, Abby. Why don't ya stay an' let me show ya round?'

'Can I, Granddad? Please?'

'All right, if it's okay with Mr Bill. I'll call back later.'

Abby stared around her dizzily as Bill led the way through row after row of pillows, stretching the length of the shop and varying in size. Some were a simple square, others rectangular, with a special heart-shaped row positioned strategically beside the counter. Most were plain white, with colour provided by a single row of washable pillows that came in bright pink or sky blue. A swinging door behind the counter led to an even larger area, off limits to customers. Sloping downwards from left to right, it was divided by three lines. In the top line and middle lines, beavers appeared to be working without supervision, while a fox wearing a pinstripe suit was seated on his own in what was the lowest line of the three.

'This is where we make our pillows, Miss Abby. See the Top Line? That's where the bags are sewn. We once had a beaver who sewed all four sides shut. Fancy that, Miss Abby! Pillow bags with no openin' left for the feathers!'

'They're such hard workers,' gasped Abby, as the beavers in the Top Line converted rolls of cloth into pillow bags at an astonishing speed.

'I should think so! Why, those workers are hen-pecked.'

Surely he had meant to say *hand-picked,* thought Abby. Knowing it was bad manners to correct someone's grammar, she bit her lip, but still the question managed to wriggle out.

'Did you mean to say hand-picked?'

'Hand-picked? Why, of course not! A duck like me doesn't even have hands.'

Abby blushed with embarrassment as Bill smiled and gestured towards the beavers.

'No, they've been hen-pecked, Miss Abby, that's for sure. Look up there.'

Abby stared in the direction of the duck's nodding head and saw a hen perched on an overhead beam. Moving her eyes back and forth, she was on a state of high alert as she kept watch on the beavers in the Top Line.

'Ya should have seen the peckin' she gave that beaver who sewed the four sides o' the pillow bag. Like poetry in motion, she was.'

'Doesn't she get tired of being up there all the time?'

'Never! She's a battery hen, ya see. That sort comes fully charged.'

Abby nodded, keeping a watchful eye on the overhead hen, as the pillow bags, now sewn on three sides, were moved from the Top Line to the Middle Line.

'This is where the bags are packed with feathers.'

'Wow! There must be millions of them.'

'This lot's fresh in from the moultin' farm, Miss Abby.'

'What's a moulting farm?'

'That's where they collect feathers from the sheddin' ducks. First they're washed an' dried, then they're weighed, an' after that they send 'em to us.'

Abby cowered in terror as a hen suddenly descended from her perch, narrowly missing her head. Her target, a beaver in the Middle Line, squealed with pain as the hen pecked at him furiously.

'He must 'ave packed in too many feathers,' laughed Bill. 'That hen's a stickler for quality control.'

Abby nodded nervously as her host led the way back to the Top Line, where the stuffed pillow bags had been returned to be sewn up. Blushing, she turned her head as Bill embraced a pillow, closed his eyes and kissed it loudly.

'This beauty's ready for the shop,' he said at length,

tearing himself away as a scuffle broke out between two of the beavers in the Middle Line. Feathers flew as they laid into each other angrily, and almost a minute passed before the overhead hen was able to restore the pecking order.

'Worth her weight in gold, that lady is,' said Bill, waddling towards the lower end of the room, where a fox in a pinstripe suit was counting a huge mountain of coins. Oblivious to their presence, he adjusted his glasses and entered some figures in a ledger, which stretched almost the length of his desk. Frowning, he erased something from a page and re-entered it correctly.

'He's a countin' fox,' said Bill. 'Why, he can add an' subtract with his eyes closed. Me? I can't abide anythin' to do with numbers.'

A trolley of pillows passed on its way to the shop and, seeing them, Bill headed for the doorway and began to flatter them amorously.

Left on her own with the counting fox, Abby shifted uncomfortably from foot to foot. The trouble with foxes, she thought, was that they always made what you said sound stupid. It was the way they looked at you, sizing you up and saying nothing. When they did talk, it was either in answer to a question or to make some point to show off their cleverness. Abby coughed to clear her throat, hoping that the fox might at least acknowledge her presence, but he continued to ignore her.

'Excuse me…' she said, finally losing patience with his bad manners. 'What is this part of the room called?'

Not bothering to lift his head, the fox pointed to a sign above his head, his demeanour making it clear that she should have known without asking. 'Bottom Line' said the sign in bright red ink.

Chapter Eight

Times were changing, thought Edgar, as he waited in his office for the arrival of the rat. If Abby should realise her dream, she would encounter a wood more complex than that faced by any previous leader. Animals were wealthier than ever before, with many now working longer hours or holding down a second job. Higher living standards had also brought demands for smoother paths, more goat police and better health care – improvements that someone would have to pay for. The beavers, not wanting to bear the cost, had taken to marching, their chants of warning ringing around the wood: 'Raise taxes and die, raise taxes and die, raise taxes and die…'

Greater competition was bringing change too, and prices were falling across the wood, with most shops giving early-bird discounts to big spenders like turkeys. Some barber shop ducks were advertising 'half off on weekdays', while in Chestnut Hill a 'Mower for Less' sign promised the kindest cut of all.

Amidst such change, no animal was under greater threat than the rat. With rival banks springing up everywhere, and the stock market competing fiercely as a provider of funds, he faced the stark prospect of having to adapt if he was to survive. The rat responded by installing rain shelters on the River Bank and providing a complimentary ferry service across the river. He then began an expansion programme, opening a succession of branches in well-appointed oak trees.

The rat also seemed to have undergone some form of personal mutation. Abandoning his former reclusive lifestyle, he became a regular attender of social events where, sporting his trademark dicky bow, he would regale guests with his tales. No longer secretive about his financial affairs, he boasted of big deals and bigger deals, many involving the takeover of other rats' banks. He also gave to charity, and was noted for his generous contribution to a home for elderly beavers near the River Bank.

'It's the rat, sir,' announced a goat guard, opening the door to Edgar's office.

'It's nice of you to call, rat. Please, take a seat,' said Edgar as his visitor was ushered in.

'Why thank you, Edgar. It's so hard to make time for friends these days.'

Edgar opened the drinks cabinet, and smiled at the rat's self-importance.

'Would you care for a little something?'

'Why, I'll join you so. Just to keep you company.'

'Of course.'

Edgar poured some port from a decanter and clinked his glass against the rat's.

'To the Great Wood!' he exclaimed.

'The Great Wood,' repeated the rat enthusiastically.

'So, how are things in the banking world?'

'Margins are tighter than ever, Edgar. But one has to look on the bright side.'

'And your family?'

'Very well, thank you. My eldest is working behind the counter. Meeting customers is the best experience of all.'

'Indeed it is.'

'Anyway, the reason I'm here, Edgar, is to support your re-election campaign. It's a personal contribution, of course.'

'That's very kind of you.'

Edgar considered the contribution, as the rat sat back twirling his dicky bow. Elections had become expensive, so much so that an eagle could no longer survive on his own resources. Billboards were now a necessity, with travel being equally essential, as personal appearances stuck in the mind and won more votes.

'I must be off, Edgar. So much to do, and so little time.'

'Well, thanks for everything.'

'Think nothing of it,' said the rat, starting to twirl his dicky bow even faster. 'That's what friends are for.'

'Well, if you ever need anything …'

The rat, having half opened the door, closed it again.

'Now that you mention it, Edgar, there is one thing.'

'What's that?'

'It's the farm bull. That crook has been going around bad-mouthing me again.'

'The farm bull? What's he been saying about you?'

'Spreading lies. Saying that I'm ripping off customers.'

'Really?'

'Yes! When we all know that he's the one who's been overcharging. I'm telling you, it's enough to make a rat's blood boil!'

'I'll certainly look into it.'

'He needs his wings clipped, does that bull.'

Edgar breathed a sigh of relief as his visitor departed, allowing him to enjoy the remainder of his port. It was typical of the rat, he thought. Who else would have sought an instant return on his donation? Still, it was soft money, and checking out the farm bull wasn't exactly a big favour.

It was later that same evening when news of Abby's collision with a falcon began to spread throughout the wood. The cause of the accident was unclear. Some blamed poor visibility, citing a pocket of fog that often hung over that part of the wood in the evening. Others said the falcon in question had an altitude problem. Whatever the explanation, Abby was seen falling from the sky before being rushed away in an ambulance.

She was unconscious when Edgar arrived at the hospital, where a team of medical foxes was battling frantically to save her. Over the next forty-eight hours her condition deteriorated further, and there seemed little hope. In the days and nights that followed, Edgar stayed by her bedside as Abby battled for her life.

'She's a fighter,' said a medical fox, shaking his head. 'It's like she's refusing to die.'

A week after the accident, Abby opened her eyes. A moment later she was asleep again, but it was a sign that the worst was over.

'She's going to make it, sir. Abby's going to be okay. It's a miracle.'

Edgar was unable to speak. His granddaughter's journey between life and death had numbed his emotions, but now the tears began to flow. In the days that followed he watched as she regained her strength, his joy tempered by the medical fox's gloomy prognosis.

'Her left wing was badly damaged by the impact of the fall, sir.'

'Are you saying that Abby won't be able to fly again?'

'It's too early to say. The damage looks irreversible, but we can't be certain. The odds are against her, sir, but we'll just have to wait and see.'

'Well, thank you for being so frank. I'm extremely grateful for everything that you've done.'

'It's an honour, sir.'

Edgar delayed telling Abby, not knowing how the shock might affect her recovery. In the end, she forced the news from him.

'Granddad?'

'Yes, Abby.'

'Do you know what I'm looking forward to most?'

'I don't know. Opening your birthday presents?'

'No, I mean when I'm better. Do you know what I'd like most of all?'

'I have no idea. But whatever it is, we must do it.'

'I want to fly to the Freedom Tower, Granddad. Like we used to. We might even see a door-to-door duck!'

'I don't know, Abby. My lungs aren't as strong as they…'

'Come on, Granddad. You can do it. I'll help you.'

Edgar took a sharp intake of breath and searched for the softest words that he knew.

'There's something I have to tell you, Abby.'

'There is?'

'You know the way that geese are always pushing themselves? Climbing mountains, going faster and further than they have ever gone before?'

'Yes…'

'Well, that's because geese never hold back. It's the only way they know. Sometimes an accident leaves them so badly hurt that they can no longer walk.'

'Why are you telling me this, Granddad?'

'When you crashed, Abby, one of your wings was broken. The doctors say it will get better, but not fully better.'

'Do you mean I won't be able to fly, Granddad? Is that what you're saying?'

Edgar nodded his head slowly, wishing that he could take his granddaughter's heavy burden and carry it for her. The freedom the Great Wood offered had come with a price, one they would now have to pay. Abby buried her face in the pillow and wept silently.

As Edgar had hoped, Abby's initial despair was soon replaced with a steely determination to rebuild her injured shoulder. Exercises, massage and weights became part of her daily routine as she did everything she could to repair the damage. Bit by bit she restored what mobility she could, but nothing she did could alter the medical fox's pessimistic outlook.

Meanwhile, in Chestnut Hill, the beaver called Bob was involved in a struggle of his own. Haunted by the memories of his flying school for birds, he was trying to content himself now that he had got his old job back again. What was it that made beavers so happy to be beavers, he wondered. Was it having two jobs instead of one? Was it spending more than they earned, especially on stuff that might come in handy in the future? Or was it eating take-away pizza and having a refrigerator full of beer?

Bob lit his pipe, and a pleasant aroma filled the room as smoke drifted from the barrel. He looked into space, and in no time at all he had the answer to his question. It was eating take-away pizza. That's what made beavers happy. Of course *he* had no liking for pizza at all, which confirmed what he had suspected all along – he shouldn't have been a beaver in the first place. What was more, ducks hated pizza too, which meant that he probably should have been a duck.

'I'm a square peg in a round hole,' he confessed to Beryl.

'What's that, dear?'

'I said I don't even *like* pizza.'

'What difference does that make, dear?'

'It means I should have been a duck, of course.'

'I wish you could just be happy with who you are, Bob. There are so many in the wood worse off than you.'

That Friday the Beaver Construction Team answered a call from the hospital, where water had leaked through a ceiling in the east wing. While searching for the source of the leak, Bob opened the door of the gym and encountered Abby doing her exercises.

'Hi, my name's Bob.'

'Hi, I'm Abby. Are you here to work on weights too?'

'No, I've come to repair your wing.'

'You have?'

'That's right. It's an emergency.'

'So how are you going to fix it?'

'The first thing we'll have to do is find the leak.'

'The leak?'

'You see, it's the water that's done all the damage.'

'It is?' said Abby, using a towel to wipe the perspiration from her forehead.

So the gym work had been a waste of time, she thought. What if all this time she had been leaking instead of perspiring? She was probably as dry as a prune on the inside, and any minute now her feathers would start to fall out. But if her wing really was leaking, why hadn't someone mentioned it before now?

'And after we've stopped the leak, we'll repair your ceiling.'

'My sealing?'

Abby had wondered about the pain in her shoulder. It always felt worse when she started to leak in the gym. If her sealing was broken, that would explain why. Abby stared at Bob and wondered. He certainly seemed to know what he was talking about, but there was something about him that puzzled her.

'Are you a doctor?'

'A doctor?' asked Bob.

'Or a wing specialist or something?'

Bob stroked his chin and looked into space. Did she really think he was a doctor or a wing something? He had played wing back once, in a charity football game, and he had a cousin who was a doctor, though there was no family resemblance that he knew of. Beryl's uncle had been a doctor, of course. That was before he ran out of patience and retired to the country. Anyway, Bob thought it was best to clear up any misunderstanding.

'I'm not a wing anything. Or a doctor.'

'You're not?'

'I'm with the Beaver Construction Team. We're here to repair the ceiling in the east wing.'

'So you're not here to fix *my* wing?'

'Your wing?'

'You see, I was out flying and I crashed into a falcon. I damaged my wing and I need to fix it.'

'Oh. I'm sorry to hear that.'

'That's okay. My surgeon says I won't be able to fly again, but I know that I will.'

'You do?'

'If you believe something enough, it will come true. That's what my granddad says.'

'Really? I've always wanted to be like a duck. Do you think I could if I believed in it enough?'

'You want to be like a duck? That's funny! I like you. You're kind of different.'

Abby laughed for the first time since her accident. She had always wanted to be an eagle, and no squirrel she ever met had wanted to be anything but a squirrel. But a beaver wanting to be like a duck – that was kind of cute.

'Can I call you Bob?'

'Sure you can!'

'Do you know what I'd do, Bob, if I could fly again?'

'What?'

'I'd fly to the top of the Freedom Tower. It's the best place in the whole wood.'

'Wow!'

'But I can't go there anymore, because of my wing,' said Abby sadly.

Bob hated to see anyone feeling sad. If only he was a wing doctor or something, maybe he could help her. Bob stared into space, and suddenly his face lit up.

'I have an idea, Abby.'

'You have?'

'*I* could take you to the top of the Freedom Tower.'

'You could? How?'

'Beavers are strong, you see. We could climb up together.'

'Wow! Are you sure?'

The following morning they set out towards the Freedom Tower. It was mid-September and the paths were draped in a leafy golden coat, which made progress slow. They had gone halfway when they were spied by a branch of squirrel youngsters.

'Where are you going?' asked the eldest, his ears cocked in readiness for their answer.

'We're going to the Freedom Tower,' said Abby, smiling at the little squirrel's boldness.

'Can we come?' said the others, rushing forward on the branch.

'No, you can't,' said Bob.

'Why not? We'll be very good.'

'Because you're not allowed,' snapped Bob.

'Why is it called the *Freedom* Tower if we're not allowed to go?' enquired the eldest squirrel brazenly.

'Because…' began Bob, stopping mid-sentence when he couldn't think of an answer.

Abby laughed as they continued on their way. She couldn't imagine anyone being able to out-think squirrel youngsters, except maybe a legal fox who would confuse them with jargon. They arrived at the Freedom Tower at lunchtime and Bob knelt on the ground so Abby could get on top of his back.

'Are you okay?' he asked, as he began to climb slowly upwards.

'I'm fine, Bob.'

They made steady progress on the first section of the Tower, a succession of small crevices giving Bob a foothold in the stone. Soon they were face to face with the treetops, and Abby stretched to her right, touching a golden leaf as it drifted away in the wind.

'Don't you just love the fall, Bob?'

'Huh?'

'The fall. The way the colours change, and the paths become so soft and leafy.'

Bob had stopped listening after the word 'fall'. Suddenly gripped by terror, he closed his eyes and clung to the stone. He had been so focused on helping Abby that the possibility of falling hadn't crossed his mind. Now he could think of nothing else.

'Are you okay, Bob?'

Then he remembered that it was the thirteenth of the month, which made matters worse. That was the date he had been evicted from his house. It was also the number of customers in his flying school for birds.

'Are you okay?' asked Abby again.

Bob didn't answer. Shutting his eyes even more tightly, he leaned forward and dug his nails deeper into the stone. With his luck, trying to stay up would be of no use anyway, he thought. Any minute now a bloody minded gust of wind would sweep him from the Tower, and he would die of shock on the way down. Or he would faint and plunge to his death without needing any help at all. Hitting the ground would kill him then, unless, like a bad cheque, he bounced and dissolved in mid-air.

Whichever way he died, they would build him back up again at his funeral service. They would say that he was a great provider, a loving partner to Beryl and a devoted father to his kits. They would duck the truth too, nobody mentioning the flying school for birds, and they would swear blind that he had wanted to be a beaver. Someone might even say that he loved pizza.

'Bob!'

Bob opened his eyes to find his funeral being interrupted by a concerned looking eagle.

'Are you afraid of heights? Is that what's wrong?'

'I'm so ashamed, Abby. I'm such a coward!'

'No you're not, Bob. It's not possible to be brave unless you're afraid.'

'It isn't?'

'Of course not. Being brave means that even though you're scared, you don't give up. You keep going, no matter what.'

Bob felt a warm glow inside his skin. Nobody had ever told him that he was brave. But Abby was an eagle, and if she said he was brave then he must be. He began to climb again, and the crevices appeared wider and the Tower less steep than it had seemed before. In a couple of minutes they were halfway up, and a little further on they reached a ledge that was wide enough to sit on. They rested for a while, admiring the woodland, which stretched as far as they could see.

'Isn't it beautiful, Bob?'

'The Great Wood? It surely is.'

'You know what you said back at the hospital about wanting to be like a duck. Were you serious?'

'Having my own business is what I've always wanted, Abby. Ever since I was a kit.'

'Granddad took me to see a duck called Bill once.'

'The pillow shop duck?'

'Yeah. He's smart, isn't he?'

'He sure is, Abby.'

'Bill said that a duck has to know what his customers really want.'

'Yeah, not like me. I started a flying school for birds once.'

'Wow!'

'It was a stupid idea. All the birds could fly already, except for a turkey who jumped off a cliff.'

'Do you know what the most important thing is, Bob? If you really want to be like a duck?'

'I dunno. Having no hands maybe?'

'It's believing in yourself. Knowing that you're the best in the wood at whatever you do.'

'Nobody believes in me, Abby. Not even Beryl. I'm not even much good at being a beaver.'

'*I* believe in you, Bob.'

'You do?'

'You're kind, and you're strong, and you care about others.'

'Yes, but...'

'And you love the Great Wood, don't you?'

'I do.'

'Well, that's what matters most of all.'

Soon it was time to start again, and they began to climb the last section of the Tower in silence. It was more difficult now, with an occasional crack in the stone being their only grip as they headed for the top. They were almost there when Bob lost his foothold and they slipped back. Clinging on desperately, they heard the debris that had come loose landing at the foot of the Tower.

'Don't look down, Bob!'

Five minutes later they had regained the lost ground, and the top of the Tower was tantalisingly close.

'Stop here, Bob. We can use the rope now.'

Abby tossed it skywards, hoping to lasso the flagpole at the top of the Tower. It fell back twice before she adjusted her position and threw it a third time.

'Got it! Come on, Bob, we're almost there.'

Bob edged his way up the last couple of feet, finding enough strength from somewhere to drag them to the top.

'We made it! Thanks to you, Bob. You're the strongest beaver in the whole wood.'

'Just as well you thought of the rope, Abby. I wish I was smart like you.'

'So now you want to be like an eagle as well as a duck! Really, I don't know what's going to become of you, Bob.'

The two friends laughed, each knowing that they would remember this moment for a long time to come. They embraced, and then Abby fell silent as she began to focus on the task that lay ahead. Looking skywards, she prayed to the Great Eagle for strength, and then it was time. Abby flexed her wings and winced as a pain cut through her left side. Bracing herself, she pushed away from the edge and immediately began to fall.

'Look out!' warned a thrush as she veered into his path,

close – Abby, the wind and the sky. Were they so close now, he wondered, that they might even be on good enough terms to speak? It was then that Edgar remembered the words of the ram seer on the day that Abby had been born: 'Tonight, an eagle will come who will one day lead the wood at a time of great need. This one, like the eagles of old, will talk to the wind and the sky.'

Edgar stared at his granddaughter, realising that destiny, ever discerning, had spared her for a reason. At that moment he knew what needed to be said.

'You are a wise and courageous eagle, Abby. One day, you *will* be the leader of Great Eagle Wood.'

Edgar's voice was heavy with emotion but, looking the other way, Abby heard only the strange enchanting notes that were drifting past on the wind. Was it the rustling of leaves, she wondered, bidding a final nostalgic farewell before going to ground? There it was again, this time flowing past in waves, and more joyful and wondrous than before.

'Can you hear it, Granddad?'

Edgar listened carefully but heard nothing, yet from the recesses of his memory he recalled a time when *his* face had lit up too.

'The music? Yes, I can hear it, Abby, but not as well as you. My ears, they're growing old.'

'Isn't it the most beautiful sound you've ever heard?'

'It's… it's one that I never tire of.'

'What is it, Granddad? Where is it coming from?'

'It's the music of freedom, Abby. Every evening, it

starts from somewhere deep inside the Great Wood. Exactly where, nobody knows.'

'Can it be heard beyond the Great Wood?'

'Some animals in other woods can hear it too. Especially when they lie awake at night with their eyes open. The music soothes their worries and their eyes start to close.'

'You mean the music puts them to sleep?'

'Yes, Abby, and gradually their sleep gets deeper and deeper.'

'Can they still hear the music?'

'Oh yes, the deeper their sleep, the more enchanting the music becomes.'

'What happens then, Granddad?'

'That's when they start to dream.'

'The music makes them dream?'

'Yes, they dream of freedom, and of a faraway wood.'

'You mean Great Eagle Wood, don't you, Granddad?'

'That's right, Abby. They dream of freedom, and of Great Eagle Wood.'

Chapter Nine

That winter the spiders of Great Eagle Wood grew increasingly restless. By day, scurrying about with purpose, they spun silky webs over vast areas of the wood. Though less active at night, they were on the move nonetheless, and frequent sightings were reported by a rabbit from the Chestnut Hill borough. Every so often they held secret gatherings, while lookouts scoured the undergrowth for intruders. Even so, a mole had burrowed a secret tunnel to break their cover, and at that moment he was listening intently as an inky black female addressed the gathering.

'My subjects, the time has come to take over the wood.'

The speaker paused, and there was a muffled roar as the assembly of spiders struggled to restrain their elation.

'We have a plan,' continued the inky black female. 'Soon, we will have control of communications and the wood will be at our mercy.'

After sustained applause the meeting continued, but the mole had heard enough, and travelling via the underground he arrived at the police station completely out of breath.

'They're going to… to… take over the… the wood.'

'Who's going to take over the wood?' asked a goat guard, stroking his beard in bemusement.

'The spiders. I heard them. They have a plan.'

'How do you know?' asked the goat guard, not looking in the least bit concerned.

'They'll control everything, that's what they said. Nothing will move without them knowing about it, because they have a plan.'

'So they have a plan,' repeated the goat guard. 'We'll see about that.'

The spiders' movements were closely monitored in the weeks that followed, but no clues emerged as to their plan, or whether in fact a plan existed at all.

'I'm telling the truth,' insisted the mole when he was brought in for questioning, accused of wasting police time.

'We've seen your type before,' said a goat sergeant, recalling a mole who had once sent him on a wild goose chase. It transpired that the goose in question, who was of excellent parentage, had merely been engaged in a spot of late-night revelling.

'But the spiders have a plan. You wait and see,' insisted the mole.

The spiders continued to be the main topic of conversation in Great Eagle Wood. Most animals agreed that they were up to something, but nobody was sure exactly what. Few believed the mole's version of events, and his warnings of plots and coups lost credibility as the weeks went by. Just when it seemed that their activities would remain a mystery, the spiders called a press conference.

'I was right all along,' claimed the mole. 'They're going

to announce their plan to take over the wood. We should flush them out now. Waiting until Friday is only playing into their hands.'

Spiders, like ducks, didn't have hands, agreed the animals, dismissing the mole's suggestion out of hand. And why, asked the goat police, would they hold a press conference if they were about to take over the wood? Nonetheless, despite what they were saying publicly, the goat police continued to watch the spiders closely.

That Friday the media centre was full an hour before the press conference was scheduled to begin. At the appointed time, the inky black female emerged from a side aisle, with a small group of companions in tow. Moving regally, she stepped towards the podium, the angle of her approach making a red hourglass marking on her abdomen visible to all. There was silence as she prepared to speak.

'Fellow citizens of Great Eagle Wood, my name is Annette. Today I bring you tidings of joy. Many of you will have seen us spiders working frantically over these last months as we set out to achieve our great aim. We are pleased to announce that we have done what we set out to do, and more. A giant invisible web now covers all of the Great Wood.'

'So that's their plan,' said the mole, nudging his companions at the back of the hall. 'They have us surrounded, and the goat police are doing nothing to stop them.'

'The giant web,' continued Annette, 'can be used to send messages to anyone, anywhere in the wood.'

All of the animals, except the mole, stood to applaud, and when the clapping died down a beaver journalist posed a question.

'How does this web work, exactly?'

'The web is made up of tiny individual strands,' explained Annette. 'Each strand is connected to a nerve centre in the middle of the wood. The nerve centre sends commands to the strands, indicating the route that each message should take to arrive at its destination.'

'And who operates the nerve centre?' asked another journalist.

Annette didn't respond, and it was clear that she was considering her answer. Standing at the microphone, her blackness contrasted with the white of the podium, her youthful appearance belying the fact that she had been four times a widow.

'My big brother looks after all of that,' said Annette at length.

'Does this web have a name?'

'It's called the wood wide web,' the black widow replied, smiling patiently as the beaver journalists wrote frantically in their notebooks.

There was mayhem in the media centre when the press conference finally came to a close. At the back of the hall, the farm bull was pressing a group of investors to go all in.

'I ain't seen nothin' like this before. Why, that web is pure magic. You want pillows? Now you can get 'em delivered to your door on this wood wide web. If ya ask me, that Annette is a widow of opportunity. I've seen plenty o' cash cows in my time, but I ain't seen nothin' like this before.'

That afternoon the web stock went through the roof. The next day it went even higher, and in the days and weeks that followed the farm bull's comments sent it higher still.

'Shoppin' malls are gonna be history, I'm tellin' ya. That web is the mall of the future. If it was my money I'd go all in, that's for sure.'

The brown bear had been away, his mood having got so black that his doctor had advised him to take a holiday. He returned to find the wood gone berserk, with almost every animal holding the web stock. Most, in fact, were still stock-piling, and beavers were mortgaging their homes to get in even deeper. Ducks, too, were buying into it, fearing that the black widow would close down their shops and drive them out of business.

As far as the brown bear was concerned, the idea of a wood wide web just didn't stack up. If you wanted to buy a pillow, you went to a shop. Spiders had eight eyes and eight legs, so they had to be good at something, but no web that he knew of could deliver a pillow. It just wasn't possible. The brown bear sighed as he struggled to make himself heard.

'It's a web of deceit. Annette is a fly-by-night operator if you ask me. That lady is heading for a fall.'

Nobody was listening, and the web stock continued its seemingly unstoppable climb. The brown bear's head began to pound and his mood grew blacker than it had ever been before. This time his doctor advised a complete rest, and he was in no condition to argue.

In Chestnut Hill, having heard rumours of vacancies at the wood wide web, Beryl was busy pressing Bob's best jacket.

'You need a second job, Bob. How else will we pay the bills?'

'You know I don't like working for anyone else, Beryl. I want to be my own boss. Anyway…'

'Anyway what?'

'Spiders give me the creeps.'

'Well, beggars can't be choosers, Bob. Anyway, spiders these days are more…'

'Scary?'

'No! More polite and pleasant.'

'Says who?'

Beryl didn't answer, and a few minutes later Bob was trudging reluctantly along Chestnut Hill in the direction of the wood wide web. What if they captured him, he wondered. He grimaced as he imagined them pursuing him through a labyrinth of webs, closing off his escape routes one by one. Sooner or later they would capture him, inject their poisonous venom and wrap him in a cocoon, ready for dinner.

'Where are you going, Bob?' shouted some squirrel youngsters, leaning from an overhead branch.

'To the wood wide web.'

'Spiders!' gasped the squirrels, moving higher in the tree.

'You can come with me if you like.'

'No way! We hate spiders. Don't we, guys?' said the eldest, scrunching up his face in disgust.

'Me too,' said Bob.

'So why are you going?'

'Beryl said I have too.'

'Our dad says spiders are yucky. He says they have eight eyes, and a big mouth to suck out your blood.'

Bob continued walking, his head stooped, more convinced than ever that he was doomed. Beryl would blame herself for having made him go, but it would be too late then, he would already be eaten. Half an hour later he reached the entrance to the wood wide web, where he was stopped and searched before being escorted inside the building. Marching him along a narrow corridor, two sentries looked neither right nor left, and Bob recoiled in horror when a long-legged greyish spider dropped from the ceiling.

'Sorry for startling you. I'm Frankie, and you must be Bob. We've been expecting you.'

Staring into as many of the spider's eyes as he could, Bob wondered whether they would kill him quickly or if it would be slow and painful like the squirrel youngsters had described.

'We're vegetarians now,' said the spider. 'Annette says it's a healthier option.'

'Oh!' replied Bob, his face turning red. 'I wasn't thinking...'

'It's okay. That's what everyone thinks. Spiders get such a bad press.'

'Yeah, you're right about that.'

'It must be our eight eyes. They seem to scare everyone.'

'Or your eight legs maybe.'

'It could be those too,' conceded the spider.

'You're a daddy-long-legs, aren't you?' asked Bob, starting to feel more relaxed.

'How did you guess?' said the spider, his mouth widening into a smile. 'Come on, I'll show you around.'

'Thanks.'

'This is the message centre,' said Frankie, opening the door to an enormous open-plan space, where spiders of all shapes and sizes were colliding as they scurried about. 'Messages from animals all across the wood are processed here.'

'Wow!'

'Annette's room is on the first floor. Up here, look.'

'What's that?' asked Bob, pointing to an even larger

room further on, where a 'DO NOT ENTER' sign was pinned to the door.

'That's where Annette's big brother works. Nobody is allowed in there.'

'It must be top secret.'

'It is. Anyway, the despatch room is back this way, Bob. That's where you'll be working.'

The despatch room was a good size, though not nearly as large as the message centre. On three sides, rows of shelves stretched from wall to wall, with signs identifying the goods that each shelf stored. In the centre of the room a transparent chute made a whirring noise as a pair of shoes slid from an overhead storage area.

'That's your job, Bob,' said the daddy-long-legs. 'To pack whatever comes down the chute onto shelves.'

That night, Bob lay awake, thinking about Annette's big brother. What secret was so secret that no one was allowed enter his room? Was it to do with the spiders' plans to take over the wood? Were they forming a secret army to lead them into battle, and establish a kingdom of spiders? No, that wasn't it. Annette's big brother had a more important reason for keeping everyone out. But what was it? Bob stared into space, and in no time at all he had the answer. Only one thing was so important, only one secret so secret, that no one else must be allowed to find out.

'Annette's big brother has the secret,' said Bob, suddenly sitting upright in his bed.

'What's that, love?' asked Beryl, keeping her eyes closed as she tried to stay asleep.

'He won't let anyone in.'

'Who won't?'

'Annette's big brother.'

'What about him?' asked Beryl, opening her eyes and stifling a yawn.

'He knows the secret,' insisted Bob.

'What secret?'

'The only one that matters.'

'What one is that?' she asked, doing her best to stay civil.

'How a beaver can become like a duck.'

'Oh, Bob, it's the middle of the night. Go back to sleep!'

'Sleep? How can I, Beryl? How could anyone sleep at a time like this?'

'You're scaring me, Bob.'

'Huh?'

'All you ever want is to change. I'm going to lose you.'

'Lose me? That's crazy, Beryl. We'll always be together.'

'Even if you start your own business?'

'Of course.'

'Why can't things just stay like they are?'

'Change helps some things to stay the same, Beryl.'

'What?'

'The wood is changing, whether we like it or not.'

'So?'

'So we must change too. As long as we do, we'll always be together, just like we are now.'

'Do you mean it, Bob?'

'Of course I do!'

'I'm such a coward.'

'No, you're not, Beryl! Abby said you can't be brave unless you're scared.'

'Abby said that?'

'She said beavers are the bravest animals in the wood.'

'She did?'

Bob closed his eyes and soon he was in a deep sleep, joining forces with the sandman, as they shared clues to unravel the big brother's secret. Beryl lay alongside, fighting the thoughts that were racing in her head. Loving someone wasn't easy, when *their* risks became *your* risks, and when they wanted to change, leaving you no choice but to follow. Beryl gasped as a shape resembling the goat sheriff floated across the room, threatening to evict them for a second time. Who would save them, she wondered, if Bob were to open another doomed business? Even if he succeeded, would it still be bad news? Besotted with his empire, would he disappear from her life as he chased the next opportunity, and the one after that? Beryl sighed with frustration, and, pulling the covers over her head, she prayed for the courage to face whatever lay ahead.

The following day Bob returned to the wood wide web, intent on discovering the big brother's secret. He spent the first hour clearing a backlog, and then waited at the end of the chute.

'It's a pillow,' he guessed, as a pair of gloves came sliding to a stop.

'It's shoes.' But Bob was proved wrong a second time when a football bounced from the chute, narrowly missing his head.

Bob, wishing that shelves hadn't been invented, stood on tiptoe and stretched upwards holding yet another pillow for despatch. By the end of the week he had tired of the chute too, blaming its constant whirring for the pain inside his head. Worse still was the fact that the big brother's room was under constant guard, making it impossible to gain entry. Bob spent the weekend convincing Beryl that he wasn't going back.

'I can't. Look at my arms! They're hanging out of their sockets.'

'Okay, love.'

'That's it! I'm not going back!'

'That's fine with me, love.'

'No one can make me.'

'Of course not.'

On Monday, Bob headed once again in the direction of the wood wide web. He was too close to give up now. Sooner or later, the big brother's room would be left unguarded, and he would discover the secret of becoming like a duck. By Friday, his shelf life was nearing its end, but when Annette announced an emergency meeting of spiders it provided the chance he had been waiting for. Avoiding the packed message centre, Bob climbed undetected to the first floor landing, and passed the black widow's room. Further on, her big brother's room came into view, its 'DO NOT ENTER' sign looking even larger than before.

Bob felt a tingle run down his spine as he stared at the sign. He had waited so long, and now he was convinced that on the other side lay the secret of how to become like a duck. Pushing open the door, Bob edged his way in and was relieved when he saw that the room was empty. Inside, a leather desk and matching chair provided single occupancy comfort, their central location allowing easy access to three rows of filing cabinets. Bob counted sixteen in all, and he was moving towards them when the sound of a voice made him freeze.

'What are you doing here?'

Bob studied the black shape which was sitting upright in the chair. Although well camouflaged by the leather, he could see that it was a spider and it was staring at him with eight eyes. Although it was a little smaller than Annette, it was nonetheless of intimidating size.

'Who are you?'

'I'm a b-b-b-beaver.'

'I can see that,' snapped the spider. 'What's your name?'

'I'm c-c-called Bob.'

'What are you doing here? Didn't you see the sign?'

'I was just…'

'Just what?'

Bob felt the hairs on the back of his neck stand up as the spider leaned towards a security button. Any second now a siren would sound, and the black widow Annette would despatch an army from the message centre to suck out his blood.

'Don't… please!'

'What are you doing here?' repeated the spider.

'I'm looking for the secret.'

'Secret? What secret?'

'Of how to become like a duck.'

'How to become like a duck? Who wants to become like a duck?'

'I do.'

'But you're a beaver!'

Bob blushed as the spider threw back his head, and his chair rocked from side to side as he laughed heartily.

'You're Annette's big brother, aren't you?'

'What if I am?'

'You don't look bigger.'

'I'm smaller actually. Male spiders generally are. But I'm older.'

'Oh.'

'That's why she calls me her big brother.'

'Can you tell me how to become like a duck?'

'How would I know?'

'Well, big brother is supposed to know everything.'

'Hmmm...'

The spider looked pleased. Usually he felt taken for granted. Now, at last, he was getting the credit he deserved. So big brother knew everything! Repeating the commendation in his head made him feel even better. So his fame had spread beyond the wood wide web, and he was spoken of by everyone, everywhere. There was probably no question that he couldn't answer.

'So do you know?' asked Bob.

'Hmm?'

'How I can become like a duck?'

It was a weird question, thought the spider. A beaver wanting to become like a duck. What *was* the wood coming to? Still, he didn't want to appear not to know. The answer would probably come to him – it usually did.

'Yes, yes! It's quite straightforward.'

'It is?'

'Why, just the other day I filed the answer in those cabinets.'

As he emerged onto the landing he was confronted by a tidal wave of legs and eyes. Standing to one side, he allowed them to pass.

'Hi, Bob,' said a daddy-long-legs, stepping out of the crowd.

'Hi, Frankie. Must have been a busy meeting.'

'Yeah, that Annette is some talker! No one can strike a chord like that lady.'

'So I've heard.'

'What brings you up here, Bob?'

'I was in her big brother's room.'

'Yeah, sure you were! Why, you two are probably best buddies!'

'I must be getting back. See you, Frankie.'

'See ya, dreamer!'

Later, as Bob left for home, he did so knowing that his task had become even more difficult. Convinced that Annette's big brother would have the answer, he had been spun everything except the secret of how to become like a duck. Straightening his shoulders and lifting his head, Bob forced himself on, believing that one day he was destined to succeed. For now, as he rounded the corner towards Chestnut Hill, that belief was all that he had.

RIVER
BANK

Chapter Ten

That Sunday, at the Freedom Tower, Bob told Abby of his experiences at the wood wide web and about meeting Annette's big brother.

'Were they scary?'

'Not at all. At first I thought they'd suck out my blood, but actually the spiders are all quite friendly.'

'Did you find out anything, Bob? About becoming like a duck.'

'Big brother said he knew the answer.'

'And did he?'

'Not really. He's a bit of a show-off. He had files about bats and beavers and stuff.'

'Was there anything about becoming like a duck?'

'There was one about *things becoming to a duck*.'

'Like having no hands, you mean?'

'That's right. And he had one about web design. That's when he got cross.'

'You know what I think, Bob?'

'Yeah?'

'Big brother just has lists of names and things. Mostly stuff that's useless.'

'You reckon?'

'Do you know what you really need, Bob?'

'What?'

'You need a role model.'

'Someone who can show me how to become like a duck, you mean?'

'That's right.'

'A teaching beaver?'

'No, not a teacher. It would have to be someone who *knows* what it feels like.'

'A duck?'

'Exactly! One that would let you work alongside him. Then you could learn what it's really like to be a duck.'

'Can you think of anyone, Abby?'

'No, but my granddad will know someone. He's smart.'

Edgar's choice of mentor was an important duck called Ronen. Of medium height and stout build, Ronen's mundane appearance masked an exceptional business brain. Where lesser ducks saw trees, Ronen had seen wood, and, hiring a team of axe beavers, he then sold the timber for profit. Soon he had built a sawmill, and then another, until eventually he was the biggest lumber supplier in the Great Wood.

'That Ronen sure is a winner,' boasted the farm bull, 'Why, that stock is goin' up so fast, it don't know the meanin' o' down.'

And so, the following Monday, Bob set off on yet another

adventure in his quest to become like a duck. On his arrival at the sawmill he was issued with a security pass, and introduced to a beaver foreman.

'I'm looking for Ronen's office.'

'It's over that way. Here, put this on and I'll take you there,' said the foreman, handing Bob a bright yellow hard hat.

'Thanks.'

The foreman led the way across a yard, and Bob covered his ears as they passed a pair of giant saws. Alongside them, beavers wearing earmuffs eyed a conveyor belt as felled trees approached in single file and offered themselves to the blades. Turning left, the foreman guided Bob through a narrow passageway, and the noise of the saws receded as they entered a building.

'Ronen's office is on the first floor. Up there.'

'Thanks,' said Bob, and he began to climb a red metal staircase, which brought him to the first floor landing. Ronen's office was straight ahead, and as Bob knocked on the door it began to slide open.

'Come on in. You must be Bob. I've been expectin' you,' said a duck, smiling broadly.

'Thanks. Nice door you have there.'

'That's a slider. Us ducks don't go in much for handles. When you've got no hands …'

'Oh, of course,' said Bob, not knowing what else to say.

'So you're the beaver who wants to become like a duck. Edgar has been tellin' me about you. He said you need a mentor.'

'I'd be really grateful. I want to start my own business, you see. I'll do anything…'

'Well, let's get started. Pull up a chair.'

Bob spent the next month finding out all about trees. He also learned about ducks and how they came up with new ideas, and he saw Ronen do deals with other ducks that made him even richer. He observed too how ducks kept the rat on their side, which gave them access to funds whenever they wanted to expand. Soon, Bob knew how ducks thought, what they ate and drank, and when they slept. In fact, he knew so much about them that he was beginning to feel like a duck himself. He also thought he knew everything about Ronen.

That was where Bob was wrong. You see, while most ducks would have been content to have such a successful business, Ronen was not that kind of duck. Deep down, Ronen was insecure, and, after many sessions on the couch, his fox psychiatrist traced the source of that insecurity to his second birthday. On that day Ronen had got twelve pieces of cake, and he ate one piece a day for twelve days. On day thirteen he went to eat another piece, but there was no more cake. Ronen cried until his next birthday, when he had his new cake cut into twenty-four pieces. That one lasted longer, of course, before eventually disappearing too.

'You can't have your cake and eat it, Ronen,' said his mother, doing her best to comfort the distraught little duck.

After that, Ronen would just look at his birthday cake and not eat it all. That way he was able to enjoy it until it went mouldy and hard. One year he got two, which was the icing on the cake, as he was able to eat one and put the other aside just for looking at.

Many years later, Ronen appeared to have put the unhappy memories of those birthdays behind him. Now a successful business duck, he could afford as many cakes as he wished. Life seemed perfect, especially as a long-awaited visit by his mother would provide the praise that he craved most of all. When she finally arrived at the giant sawmill, she was clearly impressed by what she saw.

'Look at those beavers! There must be hundreds of them.'

'Four hundred and twenty to be exact, Mum. It's one of our smaller sawmills, of course.'

'You've come a long way, son.'

'Thanks, Mum.'

Ronen smiled shyly as his mother planted a kiss on his bill. She was right, he thought. He *was* a very fine duck. Everyone said so, especially his beavers. His stock holders appreciated him too, which was no surprise considering how much money he earned for them.

'There is just one thing, son.'

'Yes, Mum?'

'Do you see all that timber?'

'Yes, Mum.'

'Well... you can't have your trees and knock them, son.'

Ronen opened his mouth to say something, but no words would come out. After his mother had gone, he began to tremble all over. That night he woke up in a cold sweat, and the following day he stayed at home with the curtains drawn. Memories of vanishing birthday cakes invaded his head when it was bright, and throughout the night the ghosts of felled trees wailed pitifully, making sleep impossible. His mother's words kept ringing incessantly in his ears.

'You can't have your cake and eat it, Ronen. You can't have your trees and knock them, Ronen. You can't have your cake and eat it. You can't have your trees and...'

Ronen started to scream. When he had finished, he started to scream again. When he could scream no more he began to think. Every day his beavers cut down thousands of trees. There were only so many trees in the wood. A time would surely come when there would be no more trees, and that time could be soon. Then his machines would go silent and there would be no more work for the beavers. The stock price would fall and everyone would blame him.

Deciding that he would have to find some other way of making money, Ronen spent the next days and nights doing nothing but thinking. He spoke out loud, too, to help him understand the problem better. Everyone knew that money grew on trees. The problem was, where else could it be found? Hardly under the ground anyway, he reasoned – moles and rabbits had been searching there for years. Birds didn't look very well off either, so there was no point in looking to the sky.

What was it, wondered Ronen, that made money, and lay *between* the ground and the sky? A moment later he realised that it was trees, and, remembering his mother's words, he started to cry.

Two days later, when he still hadn't come up with an alternative to trees, he sought advice from Bob.

'Why don't you put on your thinking cap?'

Of course, thought Ronen. Bob was right. How could he come up with the answer without a thinking cap? He searched his wardrobe and uncovered a beret he had worn to his uncle's funeral. Regrettably, although his head felt warmer, it didn't help him to think. Two football caps and a rain hat didn't work either. Then he tried the hat his uncle had worn when he was flattened by an ash, and though it helped him to think, it was only about trees.

Ronen was about to give up when, at the back of the wardrobe, he spied a wide-rimmed hat. He tried it on, and though a little loose it was held in place by a cord that fitted neatly under his bill. Ronen stood back and admired himself in the mirror.

'It's a cowboy hat,' said Bob, when he saw Ronen wearing his new hat. 'It suits you.'

From then on, Ronen began to view things differently. That night he wore the cowboy hat in bed, and the following morning he told Bob about his vision.

'There was a cloud of smoke, and all of a sudden the Great Eagle appeared.'

'You saw the Great Eagle?'

'He said I was to forget about trees.'

'He did?'

'Any old duck could make money outta' trees. That's what He said.'

'The Great Eagle said that?'

'Yeah. He said I was to make a fresh start.'

'Really?'

'Find new sources of energy, that's what He said I should do.'

'Huh?'

'Trees are a waste of time,' said Ronen, twirling the cord of his cowboy hat with his bill.

Bob shook his head in astonishment. Not being a duck, he couldn't be certain, but something told him that Ronen was talking through his hat.

The following day, Ronen recruited fifty beaver scientists to work on his new project. A week later he took on a hundred more, and as many again the week after that. Strange looking masts began to spring up across the wood, as the beaver scientists experimented with wind power, and there were angry protests from influential bird groups.

'They're a hazard,' said a falcon. 'The masts will have to go. They've already caused six mid-air collisions and at least two fatalities.'

'It's destroying the landscape too,' argued a thrush. 'Those masts are just plain ugly.'

According to Ronen, that was the cost of progress. Tree numbers were declining fast, he said, and someone had to plan for the future. Ignoring the objections, he focused on other more serious problems. Finding alternative energy was taking longer and proving more costly than he had expected. In addition, he was planning a new product launch, which would require even more funds. Fortunately, now that he had a cowboy hat, Ronen soon had the answer.

'I'm off to the River Bank, Bob.'

'But we made a double lodgement yesterday.'

'Today we're raisin' a loan, Bob. A big loan!'

'The last time I looked for a loan, they said I had no collateral, whatever that is.'

'Look around you, Bob. What do you see? Buildings? Machines?'

'So?'

'That's what you call collateral, Bob! And there's also my holding of web stock. Why, the way that Annette lady's risin', I'll have enough collateral for six loans.'

'Oh, I see!'

An hour later Ronen arrived at the River Bank. Feeling tired from the journey, he boarded the courtesy boat and closed his eyes. Once across, he was helped ashore by the single-voice swans and directed to the bank's newly extended business section.

'It's nice to see you, Ronen,' said the rat, opening his drinks cabinet and pouring from a decanter of vintage port.

'Here's to the Great Wood.'

'The Great Wood,' repeated Ronen, his cowboy hat tilting forward as he relaxed deep into his chair.

'How is the tree business?' asked the rat.

'Trees?'

The rat nodded. Having heard so much about the changes at Ronen's, he was curious to assess them for himself.

'I've seen the future,' said Ronen, sitting upright in his chair.

'You have?'

'I sure have, and there ain't no trees.'

'No?'

'Forget about them. That's what the Great Eagle said.'

'The Great Eagle said that?'

'Cuttin' down trees is a waste of time, He said.'

'Really?'

'He told me to make a fresh start. Find new sources of energy, He said.'

'And have you?'

'Well, the beaver scientists are workin' on wind power. And I've got some ideas of my own. Let me tell you about them…'

The rat twirled his dicky bow as Ronen continued his rant, and before long he was of the opinion that the cowboy duck was mad. Even so, his sawmills and web stock would still provide the bank with enough collateral for a loan. Then, even if Ronen really *was* mad, it would be no concern of the rat's.

The next day, Ronen brought Bob to a secluded spot behind the sawmill. Having checked that no one was watching, he began to talk in a whisper.

'This is where I keep my SPV, Bob.'

'Your what?'

'My special purpose vehicle. The SPV is for carrying secret loans from the River Bank. It's almost invisible. C'mon, I'll show you.'

Bob watched the cowboy duck enter the undergrowth and emerge moments later driving a strange van-like object. Built with lightweight materials, the SPV was virtually silent, and its earthy colours provided the perfect camouflage from prying eyes.

'Hop in!'

Bob stared through the tinted glass of the SPV as they rolled silently along, even managing to pass unnoticed beneath several branches of squirrel youngsters. Arriving at the River Bank, Ronen parked out of sight, and began to admire himself in the mirror.

'Who else except me has seen the future, Bob?'

'Huh?'

'What other duck has been visited by the Great Eagle?

'Huh?' said Bob, shrugging his shoulders for a second time.

'What a fine duck I am!'

Bob watched in silence as Ronen adjusted his hat to sit exactly in the centre of his head. A moment later, the cowboy duck lowered his window as a legal fox approached, carrying a folder under his arm.

'Loan terms are enforceable,' said the fox, 'subject to the party of the first part being secured by the party of the second part. Subsections 1–200 apply and, for the purposes of caveat emptor, clauses A–Z are hereby waived. Should the party of the second part…'

The fox continued, and just when Bob thought he would go on forever he stopped abruptly and passed a form to Ronen.

'Sign here!'

Satisfied that the documentation was in order, the fox disappeared, and four beavers, each dragging a trailer-load of cash, emerged from the vault. Bob helped them transfer the contents to the SPV, stacking the money under a sheet, behind a white valance that was of similar length.

'It's off-valance sheet finance,' laughed Ronen. 'Nobody will find the loan there, that's for sure.'

Having checked that the doors were secure, Ronen and Bob hopped back into the van. Half an hour later they were back at the sawmill, where they returned the SPV to its hideaway, ensuring that the loan proceeds were safe and out of sight.

Now that cash wasn't a problem, Ronen was able to hire more beaver scientists. He got his new product ready too, and on the day of its launch an impressive list of guests filled the boardroom. As usual, the duck called Bill was master of ceremonies.

'Fellow dignitaries,' began Bill, puffing cigar smoke into the air. 'I remember the time Ronen came lookin' for my advice. Tell me the secret o' business, he said, 'cause someday I wanna be a wealthy duck like you. So I said, Ronen, if you wanna be rich, ya gotta see the wood from the trees. Well now, Ronen saw the wood from the trees all right. An' after he was finished doin' that, he went right out an' sawed the trees from the wood!'

The boardroom resounded with laughter, and after Bill had finished Ronen got up to speak. Outlining the Great Eagle's revelations, he told of how he had seen the future, and that it didn't have trees. Then came the highlight of the evening and there were gasps when Ronen, flanked by three beaver scientists, unveiled his lunar-powered torch.

'This will light up every animal's life,' he said, handing one to each of the beaver reporters who were covering the launch.

Cash registers started to ring across the wood as animals queued to buy Ronen's invention. Sadly, after a bright beginning, interest faded, and some animals looked for their money back, claiming they had been kept in the dark about the torch's true capabilities. Ronen blamed a design fault,

someone else and conveniently forgetting how the lunar-powered torch had left him so light on funds. At least beavers put their hands up when they got things wrong. Then again, if ducks had hands maybe they would own up too, thought Bob, and he felt guilty for having been unkind.

'She's found them! She's found them!' screamed Ronen, banging his head against the wall in frustration.

'Who's found what?' asked Bob, scratching his chin as he tried to solve the double mystery.

'Some mole called Sher. She's found a black hole, and burrowed into my SPV. She knows all about my secret loans.'

'Oh!'

'What am I goin' to do, Bob?'

Ronen called a press conference and denied everything. He said he wasn't the only duck with an SPV, and that he had done nothing illegal. Nonetheless, with the brown bear growling about words like 'fraud', investors began to dump his stock. The rat moved to take possession of the sawmills, and, faced with mounting pressure, Ronen decided to disappear. In the weeks that followed, a cowboy hat was seen on the east of the wood, and there were numerous sightings of glow-in-the-dark sunglasses behaving suspiciously. Although the goat police followed every lead, privately they admitted that Ronen was unlikely to be seen again.

It was a sad time for the beavers and many cried bitterly as they recalled a lifetime spent working in the sawmills. Their pensions, which were invested in Ronen stock, had disappeared too, consigning them to an uncertain future. Some beavers blamed a team of counting foxes, saying that *they* should have found the secret loans.

'They were the ones paid to search the SPV,' said one beaver. 'No one knew where Ronen was getting his money. He could have been stopped if the counting foxes had found his secret loans, but they left it up to a mole to do their job. Those counting foxes are just plain greedy. We'd be better off without their kind.'

Not a shred of evidence was found to prove the guilt of the counting foxes but, even so, amid growing hostility and with the beavers continuing to castigate them, they too were forced to flee the Great Wood.

That Sunday, as Bob trudged dejectedly towards the Freedom Tower he thought of the many beavers who had worked for Ronen. Climbing without his usual concern for safety, he looked down once or twice and felt no fear. He was almost at the top when Abby appeared in the distance, the clunky beat of her wings getting louder as she drew near.

'Hi, Bob. I heard about your friends. I'm sorry.'

'They didn't deserve this, Abby. It's so unfair.'

Abby placed her good wing around Bob's shoulders, and the two friends nestled together as the wind whispered to the trees of the Great Wood.

'Abby?'

'Yes, Bob.'

'You know the way that I've always wanted to be like a duck?'

'Yes.'

'Well, I'm not so sure that I do any more.'

Abby was silent as she tried to make sense of what her best friend was saying. It had always been Bob's dream to have his own business. Now, for some reason, that dream seemed to be fading.

'This has to do with Ronen, doesn't it, Bob?'

'I'm so scared!'

'Scared of what, Bob?'

'That I could turn into a cowboy duck, just like Ronen did.'

'But you're not like him, Bob. Why, you're just an ordinary...'

'That's what Ronen was once – just an ordinary tree-cutting duck.'

'Yes, but then he changed.'

'What if I change, Abby? What if I become a cowboy duck, just like Ronen did?'

'Ronen was greedy. He wanted it all. When he put on that cowboy hat, it was *his* decision. Nobody forced him to do it.'

'That's what I'm afraid of. What if I get greedy and decide to put on one too?'

'We can all get greedy. It's in our nature.'

'That's what scares me so much, Abby.'

'But, you're a caring beaver, Bob. Remember how you carried me to the top of the Freedom Tower?'

'Yeah.'

'You risked your life for me. A cowboy duck wouldn't have done that.'

'He wouldn't?'

'Of course not! A cowboy duck only cares about himself.'

'Still…'

'It's what's in your heart, Bob.'

'It is?'

'Cowboy ducks are heartless. Sometimes you can be fooled into thinking they're just ordinary ducks, like Ronen used to be. But sooner or later you find out what they're really like.'

'Do you think it could be in *my* heart, Abby?'

'You Bob? Why, you're the kindest, most caring beaver I've ever met. I'm so proud to have a friend like you. One day your dream of being like a duck will come true, and when it does, you'll be the best the wood has ever seen.'

That night, music stirred deep inside the bowels of Great Eagle Wood. Catching the wind, it rose higher and drifted eastwards towards other woods. As usual, it told of freedom, of great deeds, and about the dream of the beaver called Bob. That night the music had a sharper, less agreeable edge too. Rising high into the night sky, it told of greed, of the cowboy duck Ronen, and of the suffering of so many beavers whose lives he had destroyed.

Chapter Eleven

Times were hard after the collapse of Ronen's business. Thousands of beavers had been left jobless, and having spent so long in the sawmills many were unable to find work elsewhere. Most animals had lost confidence in stocks too, believing that cowboy ducks had taken over the wood. Naturally enough, the brown bear was of the same view.

'There's no such thing as an honest duck,' he growled. 'Take Ronen. From the time he cut down his first tree, I knew that duck was a thief. The others are all the same. Right now, some duck is out there plotting to steal your hard-earned money. Take it from me, the brown bear won't be buying stocks any time soon. Why, you might as well be investing in a market for lemons.'

Abby became concerned, too, when animals on street corners began to point and stare as she flew overhead. She swooped lower to eavesdrop, but they would quickly change the subject and start to talk about the weather. Eventually, concealing herself on a leafy branch, she heard some squirrels say that her grandfather had accepted money from Ronen. Abby dismissed the idea as absurd. That evening, she flew to her grandfather's house and found Edgar in his study. Bent over his desk, he was holding a magnifying glass over a large, wrinkled sheet of paper.

'Ah, it's you, Abby. Come and look at this.'

'What is it, Granddad?'

'It's a map of the Great Wood, drawn before my great grandfather was born. The wood was just an open space then.'

'Were there any roads? Or railways?'

'Not at that time, Abby. At least none big enough to be shown on a map.'

'Can I ask you something, Granddad?'

'About the map? Anything you like, Abby.'

'No… it's about something else.'

'Go ahead.'

'Well, you know the way you're always helping others, Granddad.'

'Yes?'

'Does anyone ever help *you*?'

'Of course they do. Why, the beavers help every day, and the goat guards, and…'

'What about ducks, Granddad? Do they ever help?'

'Why, yes, of course.'

'So ducks do help?'

'Sure they do. Maybe not in the same way as beavers, but…'

'They give money, Granddad – is that what you mean?'

'Well, yes, a lot of ducks do.'

'Why?'

'Mostly because they love the Great Wood. You see, Abby…'

'Is there any other reason, Granddad?'

'Well, some give to the eagle they most admire. If he becomes leader, that makes it worthwhile for them.'

'Worthwhile?'

'It makes them feel they have influence.'

'Do *cowboy* ducks help, Granddad?'

'Cowboy ducks? Of course not! No eagle would take money from a cowboy duck.'

'What about Ronen?'

'Especially not from Ronen!'

Mention of cowboy ducks made Edgar bristle, but as he stared at Abby she kept her head towards the ground. No doubt she had heard the gossip, and she wanted him to tell her that it wasn't true. It was something that he could not do.

'Look, Abby. If Ronen *did* help, it was a long time before he became a cowboy duck.'

'What if it gave him influence, Granddad?'

'Influence? Ronen? Of course not!'

'What if animals *thought* he had influence?'

Edgar shrugged his shoulders, which at that moment were heavy with concern. Eagles had been involved in controversy before, one having swooped so low as to be able to eavesdrop on a rival eagle's election plans. Now, despite having done nothing wrong, they were being implicated in the murky world of political donations.

The next day, Edgar summoned the goat police chief to his office. The chief, an impressive figure, attended in full regalia, sporting stripes on both shoulders and a full set of medals across his chest.

'Have a seat, Chief.'

'Thanks, Mr Edgar.'

'Have you had any luck in catching Ronen?'

'None, I'm afraid, sir. He seems to have vanished into thin air.'

'We need something to restore confidence, Chief. This business has left a bad taste.'

'Of course, Mr Edgar. Why don't we make an example of some cowboy ducks? Maybe throw one or two in jail.'

'That won't do, Chief. We need something that will stamp out the likes of Ronen once and for all.'

'What about a badger, sir?'

'No, we need someone even tougher.'

'Tougher than a badger?'

'There's only one animal who has what it takes to do this job, Chief.'

Flattered that Edgar held him in such high esteem, the police chief straightened the medals on his chest. He had a tough image, right enough. Nobody messes with the chief, that's what they said in the force, and he did his best to live up to his reputation. Things were a bit busy at the minute. Still, if Edgar needed him to sort out the cowboy ducks, how could he refuse?

'Sir, if you really feel that I'm …'

'The animal we need is the Sarbanes Ox.'

'What?' The Chief's eyes widened in astonishment.

'The Sarbanes Ox. He's the only one who can sort out this mess.'

Of all the animals in the wood, the Sarbanes Ox was the most imposing. Hailing from Sarbanes, on the west of the wood, Sox – as he was better known – was almost eight feet tall. He sported a coat of shaggy brown fur that trailed along the ground, and a set of razor sharp horns ensured that when Sox spoke he was listened to. A tireless worker, he had an eye for detail and was trustworthy to a fault. Although generally quite patient, when provoked he had a fierce temper.

Sox got to work immediately, and together with a team of legal foxes he began to draft a set of new laws. Four weeks later a packed media centre hosted a press conference, with loudspeakers relaying proceedings to animals queuing in the hallway. Seated behind the table were Edgar and Sox, whose enormous frame stretched the chair almost to breaking point. Edgar spoke first.

'Friends, today is a momentous day in the history of Great Eagle Wood. Many of you have lost your livelihoods because of the cowboy duck Ronen. Those who bought his stock have also suffered terribly.'

There were shouts of 'Down with Ronen!' in the media centre, several rows of beavers being the most vocal.

'Our illustrious colleague, the Sarbanes Ox, is already well known for the invaluable work he has done in the past. Last month, I asked him to write new laws to protect us from cowboy ducks, a challenge which he accepted without hesitation.'

He paused as the media centre resounded with noise, with two rows of ducks, anxious to distance themselves from their cowboy cousins, cheering the loudest of all.

'The Sarbanes Ox has searched far and wide to formulate his new laws. Leaving no stone unturned, he has travelled east and west, and from wood to wood, so that we can rid ourselves of cowboy ducks.'

Edgar paused again as the beavers broke into a chant of 'Down with Ronen, down with Ronen…'

He made some closing remarks, and then asked the Sarbanes Ox to step forward. There were gasps in the crowd as Sox lifted his enormous frame from the chair. Placing his notes on the podium, he snorted into the microphone and began to outline his new laws.

'LAW NUMBER 1: DUCKS, BEING THE PARTY OF THE FIRST PART, SHALL REMAIN ORDINARY DUCKS.'

There were loud cheers, particularly among the ducks. Without so much as a mention, cowboy ducks had been outlawed, and Edgar nodded in admiration.

'LAW NUMBER 2: THE SPECIES OF BIRD ORDINARILY KNOWN AS THE DUCK SHALL NOT RAISE SECRET LOANS.'

The media centre rocked with roars of approval, and the beavers gave a sustained rendition of 'The Great Wood is great' chant. Eventually, Sox moved to quell the uproar, snorting into the microphone and rotating his head so that his horns were at their most menacing.

'LAW NUMBER 3: ANIMALS SHALL HENCEFORTH RECEIVE PROTECTION FROM FRAUDELENT ACTIVITY.'

This time there was no controlling the beavers, who left their seats to make threatening gestures at the two rows of ducks. Cries of 'Down with Ronen!' continued for several minutes. Eventually, Sox made himself heard above the din.

'LAW NUMBER 4: COUNTING FOXES SHALL NOT BE IN LEAGUE WITH, NOR CONSORT WITH, THE SPECIES OF BIRD COMMONLY KNOWN AS DUCKS.'

There were whistles and boos throughout the hall at the mention of counting foxes, only a handful of whom had decided to attend. Some beavers continued to vent their anger at the two rows of ducks.

'LAW NUMBER 5: THE SPECIES OF BIRD COMMONLY KNOWN AS DUCKS SHALL NOT PROCURE SPECIAL PURPOSE VEHICLES FOR THE SECRETIVE STORAGE OF LOANS.'

The press conference continued until all the laws, a total of thirty-five, had been announced. Sox then answered questions posed by beaver journalists, before attending a special reception hosted by the duck called Bill.

In the weeks that followed, those in breach of the new laws were hunted down relentlessly. Among the first to be arrested were identical mallard twins, who were apprehended while trying to offload a fraudulent 'no sleep' potion. Sox also ended the reign of a cowboy duck who was selling mesh umbrellas, and he called time on a peddler of silent alarm clocks. Days in jail were a useful deterrent too, and a hawker of inflatable dart boards got one hundred and eighty. Throughout it all, Sox remained unrelenting in his desire to clean up the Great Wood.

While early efforts remained focused on outing cowboy ducks, once the initial raft had been dealt with attention began to shift elsewhere. One group of beaver investors, still fuming at their stock losses, sent a delegation to meet the Sarbanes Ox.

'The farm bull told us to go all in,' said their leader. 'That black widow has magical powers, he said. Go all in and you'll be making money faster than you can count it.'

Even more serious were allegations that the farm bull had been an accomplice of the disgraced cowboy duck Ronen. He issued a series of denials, but as the evidence mounted Sox decided to indict him, citing a charge of irrational optimism. An arrest warrant was issued, and after the farm bull's initial appearance in court he was released pending trial.

No case in living memory had attracted as much attention, and as the trial date approached all eyes turned towards the Old Courthouse. On the morning of the hearing a beaver reporter jostled for position at the scene.

'Here we are, standing on the steps of the Old Courthouse, awaiting the arrival of the defendant,' he reported dramatically on camera. 'This trial, which has captured the imagination of all of Great Eagle Wood, sees the farm bull accused of irrational optimism. Any moment now he is expected to make his appearance on the concourse to our left. Let's get the views of some animals who have come along here today.'

'He should go down,' said a beaver investor, shaking his fists angrily. 'I lost everything on the web stock. The farm bull said to go all in. I want justice!'

'What about you, sir?' asked the reporter, pushing his microphone towards a badger who was shaking his head in disagreement.

'You can't blame the farm bull for other animals' bad investment decisions. He's no more guilty than I am. I think…'

'I must interrupt you there, sir. The farm bull has just arrived onto the concourse, and is at this moment walking in our direction.'

Cameras flashed as the goat police cleared a path for the defendant. Smiling ebulliently, the farm bull stopped at the bottom of the steps to answer questions.

'Is it true that the prosecution will drop the charges if you agree to leave the wood?' asked one beaver reporter.

'Wild horses couldn't get me to leave this wood,' said the farm bull. 'Why, the Great Wood has been my home since I was knee-high to a grasshopper.'

'How will you plead?'

'I'm an innocent party, an' I'm here today for one reason only – to clear my good name. Make no mistake, we're lookin' at a conspiracy here, 'cause if any animal has nothin' to hide, it's the farm bull.'

Inside, the Old Courthouse was full to capacity. It was a building of character, with a high ceiling that boasted intricate mouldings in the centre, and wood-panelled walls, one displaying a giant portrait of the Great Eagle. At the front was the judge's bench, behind which flew the flag of Great Eagle Wood. Beside the bench stood the witness stand and the desks of the court clerk and court reporter. The farm bull was placed towards the front of the main body of the courtroom, and directly opposite were the prosecution's legal foxes. In the jury box sat sixteen animals of mixed species, waiting for proceedings to commence.

'All rise,' shouted the goat bailiff as a door opened and an owl judge emerged from his chambers, dressed in a plain

The farm bull seemed surprised by the question. As far as things always going up were concerned, he had only ever thought about stock prices. There must be hundreds of other things, but what were they? He stared blankly at the legal fox, and then gazed into space.

'Answer the question, if you please,' said the owl judge.

The farm bull wondered if it was pillows. They always seemed to cost more, especially the ones with a cute cow design. Then again, prices fell during a sale. So maybe it wasn't pillows after all. What else could it be?

'Answer the question,' repeated the owl judge.

The farm bull felt himself start to overheat. Except for stock prices, he had no idea what kept going up. Unless it was fireworks! They always shot up, sometimes so high that they almost disappeared out of sight, then, when it seemed they would go up forever, they exploded and dropped all the way back down again. The farm bull snorted with frustration, blowing steam from his nostrils. Watching as it drifted towards the ceiling, his face lit up.

'I know what keeps goin' up,' he said excitedly. 'It's steam!'

The legal fox thumbed the lapels of his jacket, the expression on his face even more cunning than before.

'So steam is like stock prices?'

'That's right. Those two are regular risers.'

'Can you tell the court what happens when steam goes up?'

'It goes higher.'

'And higher?'

'Yes,' said the farm bull, looking relieved to have found the answer.

'Until?' prompted the fox.

'Until?' repeated the farm bull.

'Until it gets colder,' said the fox.

The farm bull shrugged his shoulders. He had no idea where such a tedious line of questioning was headed, and it was starting to test his patience.

'And what happens when steam gets colder?' continued the fox, a half-smile showing on his face.

'How would I know?'

'When steam gets colder, it rains.'

'So what?' said the farm bull, wondering what rain had to do with anything.

'Rain is just steam falling back down,' said the fox, his mouth widening into a triumphant grin. 'So nothing – not steam, not stock prices – stays up forever.'

There were no further questions, and as he left the witness box it was obvious that the farm bull had walked straight into the fox's trap. It was clear, too, that in relation to the charge of irrational optimism, he had a case to answer.

'Is the prosecution ready to call its next witness?' asked the owl judge.

'We are, your honour. The prosecution calls old beaver Tom.'

Two junior foxes helped a grey-haired, bespectacled beaver to get upright and shuffled him slowly towards the witness stand, where he was sworn in by the court clerk.

'Is it true that you sought advice about investing in Ronen stock?' asked the legal fox.

'That I did.'

'And whose advice did you seek?'

'His,' said the beaver, pointing a handful of shrivelled fingers in the direction of the farm bull.

'Can you tell the court what the defendant said?'

'What's that, young fella?' asked old beaver Tom, turning up the volume on his hearing aid.

'What did the farm bull say?'

'Say about what, young fella?'

'About buying Ronen stock.'

'He said Ronen was a good buy.'

'Did he say why it was a good buy?'

'Say that again, young fella.'

'Did the farm bull say *why* you should buy Ronen stock?' repeated the legal fox, having to shout to make himself heard over the buzz of the beaver's hearing aid.

'He said Ronen stock would excel.'

'And would you be kind enough to tell the court what happened next?'

'I invested everything I had in Ronen stock.'

'Everything?'

'That's right, young fella. The farm bull said to go all in.'

'And then?'

'Seven days later Ronen disappeared.'

'And you lost everything you had, is that right?'

'Yes, I did.'

'That will be all, thank you.'

'The witness may step down,' said the owl judge. 'The court will take a thirty-minute recess.'

A pair of junior foxes shuffled old beaver Tom towards his seat, as angry investors surged forward, forcing the police to form a goat shield around the defendant. Some animals swore that at that moment they saw a tear trickle down the farm bull's face; others claimed it never happened, saying it was just a trick of the light.

Edgar, seated in the main body of the courtroom, was concerned. Having heard the evidence, he felt certain that the farm bull would have to do time. What would the Great Wood do then, he wondered. There would be no good times around the corner, and the impossible would remain just that. New ideas would seem too risky and new inventions a waste of time. Glasses would be half-empty, and upsides would be downsides. It was sad, thought Edgar, that the farm bull, who had been such an inspiration to the Great Wood, now looked set to become a victim of his optimism.

The brown bear was in court too. Watching his old rival come unstuck, many believed that the bear would at last get the credit he deserved. Changing buyers into sellers, he would preside over a new era of doom and gloom, the like of which had not been seen in the Great Wood. Unchallenged, he could talk of cowboy ducks, of looming recessions, of falling profits and rising losses. There would be no bull and it would become known as the greatest bear market of all.

Failing to see the bright side, the brown bear was bent forward, his mood black and gloomy.

'I'll be next,' he growled to a companion. 'Who will they blame when some stock doubles in price? The brown bear of course. We'd have made a killing, they'll say, only the brown bear told us to sell. They'll accuse me of irrational pessimism then, and lock me up with the farm bull.'

The brown bear gave a deep growl and rose from his seat. Making his way to the front of the courtroom, he took the bull by the horns and, pulling his head forward, began to talk in his ear. Dumbfounded onlookers watched as the bull, silent for once, listened intently to what his arch rival was saying. Ten full minutes passed before the bear released his captive, giving him a thump on the back as he returned to his seat.

'All rise,' said the goat clerk, as the owl judge re-entered the courtroom.

'The prosecution may call its next witness.'

'The prosecution wishes to recall the farm bull, your honour,' said the legal fox.

'Very well. Please take the stand.'

There was an air of uncertainty as the defendant walked to the witness box and was sworn in for a second time. The legal fox had taken the steam out of the farm bull's defence – a ploy designed to show the defendant to be capable of irrational optimism – and his guilt seemed confirmed by old beaver Tom, who quoted the farm bull as saying that Ronen stock would excel and was a good buy. Now, however, following the mysterious intervention of the brown bear, there was speculation in the courtroom that something unforeseen might be about to happen.

Holding the beaver's testimony in the air, the legal fox used his free hand to thumb the lapel of his jacket.

'Old beaver Tom has said you told him that Ronen stock would excel. Is that correct?'

'I said nothing of the sort,' replied the farm bull. 'Why, that old beaver is stone deaf.'

'So you deny saying that Ronen stock would excel?'

'Yes, sir, I most certainly do.'

'If you didn't say Ronen stock would excel, pray tell us what *did* you say.'

'Why, I gave that old beaver a form, an' I said sign near the X to sell.'

'You said sell?'

'Yes, sir. Sell is what I said.'

The legal fox paused, wondering if he was hearing right. The outsize figure in the witness box *looked* like the farm bull. He even had the same voice and mannerisms. Why, then, was he saying 'sell', a word that belonged to the brown bear? Throughout the courtroom, animals stared anxiously as the legal fox planned his next attack. There was a feeling that the bull had regained some lost ground, and the next exchange could prove crucial.

'Old beaver Tom says you told him that Ronen stock was a good buy.'

'He said what?' demanded the farm bull.

'That you said Ronen was a *good buy*,' repeated the fox, waving the beaver's sworn statement in front of him.

'That's a load of bull! Look, I just wasn't gettin' through to that beaver about sellin' his Ronen stock. So I decided it was time to leave.'

'Did you, or did you not, say that Ronen was a good buy?' insisted the fox.

'I most certainly did not!'

'Then what *did* you say?'

'Why, I was past talkin' to that old beaver, so I just opened the door and said *goodbye*.'

'*Goodbye*? You said *goodbye*?'

'That's right! Goodbye is what I said, plain as day.'

The farm bull's testimony triggered noisy scenes in the

courtroom, forcing the owl judge to bang his gavel repeatedly to restore order.

'Has the prosecution got any further questions?'

'No, your honour,' replied the legal fox, a look of disbelief etched on his face.

'Very well. The witness may step down.'

After that, the farm bull put up a resolute defence, and the verdict of 'not guilty' sparked off wild celebrations in the courthouse. Some animals swore that when it was announced they even saw the brown bear smile; others claimed it never happened, and that it was just a trick of the light.

That night, from deep within Great Eagle Wood, an uplifting melody told of the Sarbanes Ox and his culling of cowboy ducks. Drifting in the wind, it spoke also of freedom and hope, and of the calming anchor that was the brown bear. Then, skipping a beat, it leapt higher, rejoicing that the farm bull had seen off his detractors and would continue to inspire the Great Wood.

Chapter Twelve

One morning that September, the Great Wood awoke to the news of a fire on the east of Chestnut Hill. Beavers stopped on their way to work and stared as fire engines flashed past, their sirens screaming. Soon, animals were fleeing for their lives as the fire gusted through the treetops, turning the sky to orange.

'The wood is on fire, the wood is on fire,' shouted a badger family, joining the exodus with whatever belongings they could carry. Beside them, animals were making a getaway using methods best suited to their abilities. Birds took flight as only they knew how, while moles were seen burrowing underground, where they would stay until the heat was off. The single-voice swans, like the ducks, took to water to escape the line of fire. Fleeing on foot, the brown bear and the farm bull were engaged in a heated discussion about their survival prospects.

'We're done for,' growled the bear, wondering whether he should bother to run or just let the fire overtake him.

'Keep movin', we're goin' to make it,' urged the farm bull. 'Why, there ain't nothin' in this wood that could outrun me.'

'We're doomed. We might as well just face it.'

'Come on, bear. Keep runnin'. I didn't escape from a farm just to end up bein' stewed alive.'

Amidst the panic, goat firefighters were bravely attacking the fire, giving ground only when the inferno threatened to engulf them. The risk was greatest when retreating uphill, their orange adversary using such occasions to quicken its advance.

'Look out!'

Firefighters ducked as the fire from the east catapulted sparks and burning debris over their heads, setting their escape route ablaze. This time there was no way out, and their comrades watched in horror as those closest to the inferno were swallowed by the flames.

Abby the eagle could feel the heat on her wings as she headed west for Chestnut Hill. From the air she spied a distraught-looking Beryl and she swooped down.

'What is it, Beryl? What's the matter?'

'Oh, Abby! It's Bob, he fell off the roof. I wanted to stay, but he wouldn't let me. You've got to help him!'

Abby flew quickly to Bob's house, where she found her friend lying in the hallway.

'Are you all right, Bob?'

'It's my leg, I can't move it.'

'Come on. I'll help you up.'

'Aaagh! It's no good, I can't.'

'Put your arm around me, I'll take your weight. Come on, there isn't much time.'

As they struggled onto the path, they were knocked back by animals fleeing from the fire.

'Wait here a minute, Bob.'

Disappearing into the sky, Abby saw thousands of animals head for the safety of the River Bank, which unfortunately Bob would be unable to reach. The media centre was a closer option, but it would involve passing too close to the path of the fire. Looking to her right, Abby saw the sky in the distance turn black, and swooping towards the ground she relayed her findings.

'Time is running out, Bob. The Freedom Tower is our only chance.'

'We'll never make it.'

'Yes we will. Come on, let's go.'

Like wounded soldiers returning from battle, the two friends leaned against each other to stay upright. Every so often Bob cried out, forcing them to stop until the pain became bearable. Further on they passed a tree of squirrel youngsters who seemed unconcerned as the traffic sped past.

'Hi, Abby. Are you in the race too?' asked the eldest.

'It's not a race, little fella.'

'Is it a treasure hunt? Can we go with you? We're ever so good at finding things.'

'Where are your mum and dad?'

'They're gone shopping. We're getting nuts, aren't we, guys?'

'The wood is on fire. It's not safe here.'

'What's a fire, Abby?'

'It's when everything gets really hot.'

'That's cool! Did you hear that guys?'

'Look, you'll have to leave.'

'Can we come with you, Abby? Can we?'

Abby searched among the sea of faces milling past and eventually recognised a badger, who stopped when she called out.

'Can you help these little squirrels?'

'Sure thing, Abby. Hop on, guys. I'll take care of you.'

Abby and Bob continued on their way, aware that although the fire's advance seemed to have slowed slightly, it was still rampaging through the wood.

'There's the Freedom Tower, Bob. Come on, we're going to make it.'

The last half-mile seemed to take forever, and Bob's hair was matted with sweat as every movement sent pain shooting through his leg. Finally they reached the Tower, where Bob collapsed in a heap, with an exhausted Abby slumped alongside him. Lying there, the little eagle listened as the fire from the east drew ever closer, and a tear trickled from her eye.

'You know something, Abby?'

'What?'

'If this hadn't happened, I think I could have done it.'

'Done what, Bob?'

'Started my own business. And you know why? Because you made me believe in myself.'

'Don't give up yet, Bob. We can still...'

'There's one thing I want you to do for me, Abby.'

'I'd do anything, Bob. You know that.'

'I want you to promise that one day you'll become the finest leader the Great Wood has ever had.'

'Bob...'

'Thanks, Abby. Thanks for everything.'

'Look, we can climb the Tower. At least let's...'

'You must go now, Abby, while there's still time.'

'I can't, Bob. Not when…'

'Go on! You have to.'

The best friends embraced, and then, pushing her away gently, Bob sent the little eagle on her way.

Abby flapped her wings, and without looking back she flew towards the sky. From there, she judged the fire to be an hour away at most. Using air currents to drift higher, to the east she saw only a ball of fire, and even the river, its waters strewn with fallen trees, looked to be ablaze. Abby gasped when sudden turbulence threw her off course, flinging her first one way and then the other. As she recovered, the wind laughed in her face.

'How dare you!' shouted Abby, as she was swept upwards again and tossed around until she was breathless with rage.

'You're just a bully!' she screamed. 'Anyone could out-blow an eagle, especially one with a bad wing.'

The wind remained still, considering the accusation, and it was about to blow its top when Abby got in first.

'I know someone who can blow stronger than you!'

Still silent, the wind searched its memory for the name of one so powerful. Sometimes, when warmed by the sun, it scarcely had the strength to blow, certainly not in the cold way that it liked. But then there were times when *it* was the master, and if angry, it could raise sandstorms that blocked out the sun. So who claimed to hold sway over the wind? Making circles above the Freedom Tower, the wind whistled the question into the air.

'Whooooo…?'

'The great fire from the east,' replied Abby. 'It says there is no one mightier, not even the wind.'

The wind emitted an angry gust, and began to head eastwards towards the great fire. Howling defiance, it forced trees to give way, their leafy dresses curtseying as it whirled past. From a distance, the wind's rival saw it approach and, lowering its head, prepared for war.

'Wham!'

The great fire from the east buckled under the force of the impact. Then, finding its second wind, it weathered the storm and began to move forward again, though more slowly than before. From a distance, Abby watched the wind rage, yet still fall short of landing a telling blow. The time had come to seek help from an even higher power.

Opening her wings, Abby began to climb. As she rose, the detail of the Great Wood began to fade, the distance lessening even the menace of the fire from the east. Abby's muscles ached with the effort, yet she continued her ascent, grateful for the cooling air that fanned her wings. She was higher than she had ever been before, but still she kept climbing, ignoring the pain.

'That's high enough!'

Abby stopped, and felt every sinew in her body cry out. Forcing out the words, she told of the plight of the Great Wood.

'It's burning us!'

'It's burning *you*,' replied the sky.

'But don't the sky and the Great Wood look out for each other?'

'Not any more. The sky only looks out for itself now.'

'Don't you care about the Great Wood any more?'

'Why should I? The Great Wood doesn't care about me.'

'Are you crazy?' shouted Bob, having to crawl to escape from the fumes.

High in the sky, Abby watched her fire move steadily eastwards, its fledgling enthusiasm compensating for an obvious lack of maturity. After fifteen minutes it had burned some distance from the Tower, its appetite eating it closer to its rival, which was continuing to blaze a trail westwards.

Ten minutes later the fire from the east caught sight of the rival that Abby had sent to battle it. Stifling a laugh, it boasted of felling a forest of trees, of defying the wind and of resisting the fire brigade from the sky. Determined to earn its place in the hall of flame, the fire from the east gave a mighty roar and lowered its sights as it prepared for war.

Despite the odds, Abby's youngster was advancing steadily, showing a burning desire to prevail. Only a half a mile of ground now separated the contenders, as they readied for the fray. Five hundred yards to go... four hundred... two hundred... one hundred... Abby felt the heat rise from the ground and saw the gap disappear as the firebrands rushed to embrace.

The flames rose on impact, then immediately fell back as the youngster imploded, cut through with impunity by the great one from the east. Abby watched in horror as the victor advanced, the Freedom Tower now firmly in its sights.

'I can't stop it, Bob! I've failed you. I'm so sorry.'

'Don't be, Abby. You did everything you could.'

Then, with destiny beckoning, the great fire suddenly began to struggle. Was its resolve weakening, wondered Abby, or was it finally noticing the wind in its face? Perhaps the delay was simply a ploy, as it made ready for a final assault on the Tower. Or had her youngster, though seeming only to inflame, inflicted more damage than she had thought?

The fire from the east staggered forward and began to gasp for air. Abby and Bob watched it battle to stay alive as the sky continued to pour water on its hopes.

'It's dying, Abby. There's nothing left for it to burn. Your fire has eaten everything between it and the Tower.'

Searching desperately for a lifeline, the fire from the east launched sparks and debris towards some trees beyond the Tower, but the wind held firm and blew them back in its face. After a day of terror, of wreaking havoc and destruction and taking so many lives, the fire from the east had burned itself to a standstill.

'You did it, Abby! You saved the Great Wood.'

'Sometimes you must fight fire with fire, Bob. When there's no other way.'

An investigation into the cause of the blaze got under way, even as embers from the great fire were still glowing across the wood. Some animals were blaming Ronen, saying it was either an act of vengeance, or another of the cowboy duck's misfiring inventions. The mole was holding the black widow responsible, claiming it was part of Annette's fiendish plan to take over the wood.

With a large number of hawks patrolling the skies over the Freedom Tower, speculation mounted that the fire had been started maliciously. Time-honoured protectors of the Great Wood, the hawks were always to the fore in times of danger. Trained and fearless assassins, even those reduced by age stayed active through their aggressive support for bloodshed.

That evening, Edgar attended a gathering in the House of Eagles, where an air of gloom hung over the great hall. Every species of animal was represented, the fire having brought suffering to them all. As usual, there were two rows of beavers at the back, and, in an impressive show of solidarity, a full line of senior hawks sat towards the front. With flags at half mast, Edgar moved onto the stage, and his voice shook with emotion as he began to speak.

'We began this day, my friends, full of hope and confidence. Fall is a time for reflection, when the old gives way and we await the dawn of new beginnings. For those cut down by the fire from thc east, that dawn is lost forever, and today we mourn our lost comrades.'

Edgar paused and there was silence in the great hall as the animals bowed their heads and remembered their loved ones.

'Today we especially salute our goat firefighters, so many of whom gave their lives in the cause of the Great Wood.'

There was sustained applause in the House of Eagles as the animals paid tribute to the courage of their fallen comrades. There followed a respectful silence before Edgar continued.

'There is somebody else whose courage and resourcefulness prevented many more lives from being lost, someone who, when the need was greatest, fought fire with fire.'

There was a huge cheer as Abby appeared on the stage and was presented with the Great Wood's medal of honour. As she returned to her seat, the goat police chief approached the podium, whispered something to a visibly shocked Edgar, and began to address the crowd.

'Today, there have been three fires in the Great Wood. One, which started in the north, was quenched by our courageous firefighters. A second fire in the east caused untold devastation and loss of life. An attempt to start a third fire was foiled by a brave group of beavers, who unfortunately perished along with the arsonists.'

There were gasps in the great hall, and it was several minutes before the police chief was able to continue.

'We have evidence that all three fires were started by racoons from a faraway wood.'

There were angry cries and the beavers at the back took up a chant which spread throughout the hall.

'Some woods are bad, some woods are bad, some woods are bad...'

Edgar called for calm, but he was shouted down by the most senior of the hawks.

'This is war! Tonight we must march against the racoons and teach them a lesson they won't forget.'

There were raucous cheers as animals screamed their support for the hawks, the beavers shouting 'Death to racoons, death to racoons...', a chant that was taken up throughout the hall.

Nobody did war better, thought Abby, observing the hawks' skill at working the crowd. Was war the answer, she wondered. Would it stop other racoons intent on similar missions of death? Would fear force them towards peace, or would their own hawks simply use it to fuel further hatred of the Great Wood?

Abby waited a while longer, hoping that someone would protest, but the hawks, now orchestrating the beavers' chants, had control of the hall. Moving onto the podium, she felt her body tremble as she leaned towards the microphone.

'Stop! Stop!'

She said it over and over, until she was heard through a lull in the beavers' chants.

'What?' shouted a senior hawk, standing defiantly in the centre of the hall.

'Invading other woods hasn't helped,' said Abby, her heart thumping as she stared at the stunned faces.

'We haven't even sent our army yet!' shouted the hawk angrily.

'The Great Wood doesn't need an army to invade.'

'What?' thundered the hawk.

'Every night, our music drifts in the wind and tells of freedom and hope.'

'So we've been invading them with music?' suggested the hawk.

'That's right, and when other animals hear it, they want their wood to be like the Great Wood.'

'So what's the problem?' demanded the hawk.

'Some woods don't want to be like us. They just want to stay the way they are.'

'So they set fire to the Great Wood because they don't like our music?'

'Exactly!'

'Rubbish! She's talking rubbish,' screamed the most senior of the hawks. 'I say we attack tonight. Let's send an army to teach them a lesson.'

There was mayhem in the great hall as animals took sides, the ducks supporting Abby, while the others seemed mostly to side with the hawks. At the back, the beavers broke into a sustained chant of 'Some woods are bad, some woods are bad…' and, after several attempts to restore calm, the meeting broke up in disarray.

That night, high above the Freedom Tower, the sky comforted the Great Wood with a blanket of love. Amidst its sparkle, it remembered the gutsy little eagle who said that she cared, and it knew that she was the brightest star of all. Further down, the wind too was out and about, rustling through the branches and boasting of having single-handedly blown away the fire from the east.

No music came from the Great Wood that night. Instead, a primeval scream of anguish rose deep within its bowels and asked '*why?*' Floating sorrowfully on the wind, it told of suffering and pain, of wanton destruction and immense loss. There was a cry of raw anger, too, as the Great Wood vowed that whoever had unleashed the fire from the east would be made to answer.

Chapter Thirteen

Great Eagle Wood was on red alert in the days that followed, with most animals, fearing further attacks, opting to stay in their homes. Those who did venture out faced long delays at police checkpoints, as the search continued for those who had masterminded the fire from the east. Edgar the Eagle was a visible presence as he visited the injured in hospitals and toured the wood to inspect the damage. Wherever he went, a retinue of senior hawks was close at hand, and though his eyes were bloodshot and his frame frail and unsteady, the old eagle did what he could to comfort and reassure the Great Wood.

Amidst the carnage, stock prices, which had plunged, were staging a modest recovery. The farm bull said it wasn't the first time that something bad had come from the east.

'Those racoons aren't goin' to bring this wood down, that's for sure. Right now, we've all just gotta do our bit. Every one of us should be out there buyin' somethin'. Why, we'll have this wood back on track in no time.'

As the rawness of the racoons' attack receded, a steady trickle of families began to return to their homes. Among them was Bob who, having discarded his crutch, was walking with a limp. Beside him, Beryl was silent as they rounded the corner on Beavers' Grove, where missing landmarks were a poignant reminder of the fire from the east. It was no different at Chestnut Hill, where a construction team was removing the remains of trees that had lined the path. Despite the extent of the devastation, Bob and Beryl were still unprepared for their arrival at number 12. Their cottage, now de-thatched, had caved in at the roof, filling the inside with debris. The windows, which were pane-less, had suffered too, their bent frames mercifully obscuring the blackness that lay beyond. Bob opened the charred door enough to see inside and watched helplessly as Beryl broke down in tears.

'Look at our beautiful cottage, Bob. It's destroyed!'

Comforting his distraught mate, Bob promised to make good the devastation, and with the help of the Beaver Construction Team he soon had the cottage restored to Beryl's satisfaction. Winter passed and life began to return to normal, as spring brought growth and renewal throughout the wood. Even so, hawks still patrolled the skies, their presence a constant reminder that the fire from the east had not been forgotten.

Having attended to everyone else's needs following the great fire, Bob began to retreat into himself. On weekdays he left Chestnut Hill only to go to work, and at weekends he was rarely seen outside number 12. That Sunday, however, he agreed to meet Abby at the Freedom Tower, where he confided in his friend how he was feeling.

'You know the way you saved my life?'

'Yes, Bob.'

'And my leg is better and I have a good job?'

'Yes.'

'I should be happy, shouldn't I?'

'And are you?'

'Not really, Abby. For some reason, things are getting me down.'

'I think I know why, Bob.'

'You do?'

'It's because you still want to be like a duck. That's what's making you feel bad.'

'Do you think so?'

'I know so, Bob. You've always wanted your own business. Dreams don't just go away, you know.'

'Do you think it will ever happen, Abby?'

'Of course it will. But you've got to keep believing in yourself, Bob. Then, everything is possible.'

Bob felt like a new beaver as he left the Freedom Tower. Believe! It was what he had to do to become like a duck. Abby had said it, and she was always right. At that moment Bob began to believe that he was the smartest beaver in all of the Great Wood. Passing the duck called Bill's shop, he wondered if Beryl would like one of the red pillows. She had a small head though, which meant that the brown one might suit better. Then there was the yellow one with the ribbons. Bob scratched his head, thinking that maybe he should buy her flowers. If Beryl didn't like them, at least they would wither and die, but the wrong pillow would last forever.

'Believe!' said a voice in his head, persuading Bob to take another look at the pillows. Yes, Beryl would be pleased. He could see her now, praising his choice as she cooked him something special for tea. I have a mate in a million, she would say, making him blush with embarrassment. Bob stared at the window. Pink was Beryl's favourite colour, and it was good value too. But would the green go better with their walls? Pale blue was a possibility too. He was about to choose between orange and yellow when he remembered the time he had bought hats for their beaver kits. They were too shiny, Beryl had said, warning him never to buy anything again.

Deciding against the pillows, Bob went in search of flowers instead. Further on, he noticed a sign above a shop advertising 'Re-tail Therapy', and Bob scratched his head wondering if it meant what he thought. Beryl's tail hadn't been the same since the trauma of the great fire. Fixing it would be worth more than pillows and flowers put together. Bob walked towards the shop and joined some she-badgers queuing on the sidewalk.

'I get mine done at Claude's,' said one, removing a glove and flashing her nails.

'I wouldn't go anywhere else,' agreed her friend.

'It's so hard to get good therapists these days,' complained the first badger.

'You're right there,' replied her friend. 'Why, only the other day I came out in a rash after a facial.'

Bob hid his nails, and tried hard to make the rest of himself invisible too. He was doing it for Beryl, he thought, as he watched a badger stare at him and turn up her snout. Anyway, if he left now, they would talk about him. Leaning against the shop window, Bob levered himself into a long-stay position and made it clear that he wasn't leaving.

'The class of animal you meet nowadays!' remarked the first badger to her friend.

'You're right, Clarissa. It's a disgrace!'

The queue seemed to take forever to get inside the shop but, having committed himself to the wait, Bob held his ground. He felt his face turn red as Clarissa scrunched up her nose and began to sniff in his direction.

'What's that nauseous odour?'

'Hard to say, Clarissa. It reminds me of…'

'Skunk?' suggested Bob, trying his best to be helpful.

There were gasps in the shop, and several of the badgers jumped onto the counter, leaving the rest to seek refuge wherever they could find it. As the panic subsided, all eyes turned towards Bob.

'The smell is from him. It's beaver pong,' said Clarissa, prompting a collective sigh of relief in the shop.

'Do you know how long it takes to get rid of skunk scent?' asked another she-badger.

'Two days?' suggested Bob, reckoning it had to be a long time or otherwise she wouldn't have asked.

'Two days!' exclaimed the badger. 'Did you hear what he said? Two days!'

The she-badgers laughed heartily, almost warming to Bob, who was glad he wasn't a skunk.

'Two *years* it took my grandmother,' insisted the badger at the front. 'Two years to get rid of skunk scent. And she used to wash four times a day.'

Eventually, Bob reached the top of the queue, where a

bespectacled beaver was taking deposits and writing dates into a book.

'When would you like to book in for, sir?'

'Book in?'

'For re-tail therapy, sir. When would you like to have it done?'

Bob stared at the beaver, who was waving his pencil above the appointment book, awaiting a decision.

'What's re-tail therapy?' asked Bob.

'It's to make you feel better, sir.'

'But I feel better now.'

'You see – it's working already, sir.'

'Make up your mind,' said a she-badger who was third or fourth in the queue. 'We can't wait forever.'

A security goat appeared from behind the counter and beckoned to Bob, who followed him towards a door that opened into a smallish room. Inside, seated at a table, was a round-faced duck wearing a wide-brimmed hat.

'Sit down, sir. How can I help you?'

'What exactly is re-tail therapy?'

'Well, it's usually females who get it done, especially badgers. Spendin' money just seems to make them feel better.'

'But what is it?' insisted Bob.

'First of all we snip off their tail, a painless procedure done under anaesthetic. Then we re-shape it. We have forty different designs. Sleek is our best sellin' range, though bush is popular too. Dyein' is optional, an' then it's simply a matter of sewin' it back on.'

'Sewing what back on?'

'The tail, of course!'

Bob felt his tail and knew instinctively that it was intended to stay put. Anyway, there was no way Beryl would consider anything that involved risk.

'You're a cowboy duck, aren't you?'

'No I'm not,' said the duck smiling.

'Yes you are.'

'Okay, okay, what if I am?'

'You're just taking the badgers' money.'

'But re-tail therapy is good.'

'It doesn't even work.'

'That's not the point. Feelin' good is what matters, an' that's what spendin' money does. Re-tail therapy is good, believe me!'

'I don't know.'

'What's your name?'

'Bob.'

'*You* could make the she-badgers feel good too, Bob.'

'I could?'

'All you'd have to do is help us snip off their tails.'

'But I'm not a doctor.'

'Who said anything about a doctor?' replied the duck, smiling so that his face looked even rounder than before.

'Is it hard?'

'It's simple,' said the duck, his cowboy hat shifting on his head as he grinned even more. 'Why, I'd do it myself if I had hands.'

'I don't know.'

'Well, that's okay. But if ya wanna be like a duck...'

'Like a duck?'

'Sure! We'd be partners, Bob. I'd do the sellin' and you'd do the snippin'.'

Bob stared into space and wondered. Was re-tail therapy good, like the duck said? Spending money certainly

'Hey, that's close! He's pretty smart for a beaver, Miss Abby.'

'It was just a guess,' said Bob modestly.

'Well, we went and sold 'em for pillow fightin'. No one's ever lost with one o' these beauties! Ya see, Bob, when somethin' ain't sellin,' it's all about marketin'. If ya don't have what the customer wants, ya gotta make the customer want what ya have!'

'*You know what,* Abby?' said Bob, as they left for home, 'I'd only ever want to be like a *real* duck.'

'I know that, Bob.'

'I was thinking… '

'Yes, Bob?'

'About what the duck called Bill was saying.'

'What was that?'

'About marketing.'

'Yeah?'

'Well, you know my flying school for birds?'

'What about it?'

'Well, almost everyone likes spending money, right?'

'Yeah, especially badgers.'

'And Bill said that if you haven't got what the customer wants…'

'… you've got to make them want what you have.'

'Exactly!'

'Exactly what?' said Abby, shrugging her shoulders.

'You see, instead of a flying school for birds, I need a…'

'A what, Bob?'

'A school for flying birds!'

'A school for flying birds?'

'Can't you see, Abby? Every bird that can fly will want to join. And that means *every* bird.'

'I don't know, Bob. What if…?' Abby listed all the reasons why the school wouldn't work. It was the wrong time of the year, she said, and birds, being prone to flights of fancy, were unreliable customers. The excitement drained from Bob's face as she continued to find fault and, seeing his head drop, Abby felt ashamed.

'I'm sorry, Bob.'

'What?'

'I was just jealous.'

'Jealous?'

'You see, eagles always want to be the ones to come up with new ideas.'

'That's okay, Abby.'

'You know something, Bob?'

'What's that?'

'The whole wood is going to be talking about your flying school.'

'Really?'

'And you want to know something else?'

'Yes?'

'You're going to become like a duck, Bob! Just like you've always wanted.'

This time Bob did his homework, and every bird interviewed said the flying school would take off. Bob secured a site to the west of Chestnut Hill, and enlisted the help of the

Beaver Construction Team to get the building work under way. As the weeks passed, news of the flying school quickly spread, with membership details being carried on the wood wide web. Seeing its potential, the rat was on board immediately, twirling his dicky bow as he advanced funds for the construction work. The biggest admirer of all was the farm bull, who was so excited that he was snorting steam from his nose.

'It's goin' to be some take-off, par'ners. Why, every bird that has feathers is goin' to be joinin' this school. The sky had better be on the lookout, 'cause this one's headin' straight up! If I were you, I'd go all in, an' just hang on for the ride.'

The brown bear was not impressed. Covering his head, he gave a long sigh, saying that he'd seen it all before.

'Hah! This school will be giving lessons about how to lose your money,' he growled. 'It's heading for a crash landing, just you wait and see.'

Membership was full long before the flying school was ready to open, and Bob, encouraged by his success, was already eyeing the next opportunity. Back in Chestnut Hill he paced the kitchen floor excitedly, telling Beryl of his plans.

'This is only the start.'

'What do you mean, Bob?'

'Birds nowadays have lots of money, right?'

'I don't know…'

'Every one of them has a nest egg. Even the rat says it.'

'Okay, so they have some money, Bob. But what difference does that make?'

‘They can only spend so much on flying, right?’

‘Okay…’

‘And once it gets dark they’re grounded.’

‘So?’

‘So then they need something else to do.’

‘Right.’

Beryl nodded as she tried to take in the full significance of what was happening. Bob’s imminent success meant that he would soon become like a duck, and she was pleased for him, and even a little proud. They would move house, have a workforce of beavers and be the envy of Chestnut Hill. As the opening of the flying school loomed, however, Beryl was aware that there was no such thing as a free launch. She would have a bigger house, but would see less of Bob, as he became consumed by the business. A tear fell from Beryl’s eye and rolled the length of her face as she remembered their early days, when they had been so much in tune. Bob had put her before everything back then, as they enjoyed each other and put time into their kits. Things were different now, she thought, and there was no going back. Taking a tissue from her bag, Beryl wiped away the tear and wondered if she would be able to cope.

A month later Bob’s business was up and flying. Throughout the day, a steady stream of traffic took to the skies, the falcon who had collided with Abby being the first to register on the ‘air miles’ programme. By night, business moved indoors, the members’ area offering dining facilities, while a ‘full house’ sign at the card school promised the best deal of all. On the stairs, beavers hurried past, ferrying towels for the bird bath located in the leisure complex. The crow bar, in the public area, was Abby's idea, and there a resident thrush played the piano, with a warbler and two hummingbird sisters providing the vocals.

In the centre of the dance floor, two females were vying for the attentions of an obviously desirable male.

'It's my tern!' insisted one.

'I saw him first. He's my tern.'

'Let go! He's mine!'

It fell to the bar manager, Jack Daw, to pull them apart, before introducing the act that was top of the bill.

'Males and females, the school for flying birds searches far and wide to bring you the very best in live entertainment. This evening is no exception. Please welcome the wood's very own stand up comedian: the Raven Lunatic!'

Later that month, the reported sightings of racoons meant that security was tight for the school's official launch. Birds, exercising their members' rights, occupied two rows to the left of the stage, with a group of senior owl judges completing a front bench of who's who. On the right, the farm bull and the brown bear were each allocated a double space, as was the Sarbanes Ox, who was seated next to the rat.

Elsewhere, beavers, following Bob's lead, were mingling with the crowd. Some, conversing with ducks, were putting forward business ideas of their own. Others were talking to foxes, who, smiling slyly, were revealing as little as they could. One beaver with leadership aspirations had managed to corner an eagle, while his friends were networking with anyone claiming to have influence.

On the stage, with Beryl and Abby at his side, Bob was shifting about nervously. So much had happened since he had first wanted to be like a duck. Thanks to Abby, now it was about to come true. The sound of police horns marked Edgar's entrance, and along with his retinue of senior hawks, he was shown to a seat beside the flag. His arrival was the cue for proceedings to begin, and, forcing his bloated frame upright, the duck called Bill waddled towards the microphone.

'Mr Edgar, birds and animals of the Great Wood, today belongs to the beaver called Bob.'

There was a huge cheer, and the beavers at the back began to shout 'The beaver called Bob, the beaver called Bob…' for several minutes before Bill was allowed to continue.

'Bob once came to me and said he wanted to be like a duck. This was fancy talk, I said, comin' from a beaver, but he just wouldn't take no for an answer. So I said, Bob, you need two things to start yer own business. First, you gotta be sellin' somethin' that a lot of animals want. Like pillows, I said, everyone needs pillows. Now, I said, there's just one more thing you've gotta do, an' that's to watch the *bottom line.* 'Cause if yer goin' to stay in business, Bob, ya gotta make a profit! I…'

Tiring of the rambling address, the beavers again took up the chant of 'The beaver called Bob…' and it took the intervention of the goat police to restore calm.

'I now call upon Abby,' said the duck called Bill.

Rising from her seat, Abby winked at Bob as she walked towards the centre of the stage. Adjusting the height of the microphone, she spoke in a strong voice.

'I am standing here because of a friend who once risked everything to keep my dreams alive. That friend had a dream too, and despite facing setbacks and misfortunes, he always believed that it would come true. Today it has, and the beaver called Bob, who has long dreamt of becoming like a duck, has realised his dream.'

There was a spontaneous burst of applause, and the animals of the Great Wood rose to salute the humble beaver who had dared to dream. On the stage, Bob's eyes filled with tears.

'My friends,' continued Abby, 'many years ago the Great Eagle created this wood in His own image. Today, as He smiles down on us, He is saying well done, animals and birds of the Great Wood. You have lived, as I ordained, in peace and harmony, each for the betterment of one another. You ducks, the risk takers, have created opportunities, with beavers working tirelessly at your side. Your endeavours have been funded by the rat, and your paths smoothed by the counting and legal foxes. Sagging spirits have been lifted by the farm bull, and feet kept grounded by the brown bear. I salute you goats, who work so selflessly in the service of the Great Wood, and the countless geese, whose spirit of adventure continues to sweep us to new frontiers. To the spiders, spreaders of the word, long live your wood wide web. Lastly, I salute you eagles, who have been loyal and true servants, and who have led the Great Wood with vision and purpose.'

A chant of 'The Great Wood is good, the Great Wood is good…' went up from the beavers, and Abby sipped some water before continuing.

'Friends, we stand here today, a free wood, a wood that has faced every challenge with fortitude and resolve. The fire from the east, sent to weaken us, has served only to make us stronger. We go forward, protecting our wind and our sky, and respecting the rights of other woods. In the Great Eagle we trust.'

There was a tremendous outburst of applause as Abby left the microphone and embraced the beaver called Bob. Then, turning to Edgar, she held the old eagle close and whispered in his ear.

'You're still my hero, Granddad.'

'And you're mine.'

'Let's go to the Freedom Tower. One more time.'

'I don't know, Abby. It's such a long way.'

'Come on, we'll go together, like we used to.'

Waving the hawks aside, Edgar got slowly to his feet and began to stretch his wings. A minute later he was airborne, but only just, as he rose a little and battled for parity with the tree tops. Turning to Abby, he tried to talk but found his breath held in by the stiffening breeze.

'Can you help us, please?' said Abby, and the wind, hearing her, changed direction and went with them.

'Thanks,' said Abby, 'I knew you would.'

They flew downwind then, and rose a little more, though under the thickness of the cloud cover Edgar still struggled for breath.

'Can you help too?' asked Abby, and the sky, without answering, began to clear, and soon the air was easier to breathe.

'Thanks,' said Abby again. 'You're a star!'

They rested once or twice along the way, and as Edgar grew tired the wind stiffened to help him.

'You made it, Granddad! I knew you would,' said Abby, as they glided in and landed on the Freedom Tower.

'Never again,' wheezed Edgar. 'My lungs are gone. Only for the wind, I wouldn't have made it.'

'Isn't it beautiful, Granddad?'

'Yes, from here, you can see everything, which is what eagles do best.'

'See the big picture, you mean?'

'Yes, knowing that if one beaver breaks the mould, others will follow.'

'You mean Bob, don't you?'

'You set him free, Abby. Real freedom comes from within, and when Bob became like a duck, it unlocked more chains than any army of hawks.'

'You would have done it too, Granddad. It's an eagle's job.'

'Yes, our role is to lead. That's why the animals look to us.'

'You're the best leader ever, Granddad.'

The old eagle smiled, and the wrinkles softened and spread across his face. He had lived a long time, seen many changes, and he had done his best for the Great Wood. Now, he was tired, and he knew that it was time.

'I'm getting old, Abby.'

'Don't say that, Granddad.'

'I can't go on forever. Soon, the wood will need a new leader.'

'But, Granddad…'

'It must be someone who loves the Great Wood. Someone who will stand up to the hawks, care for the animals, and look out for the wind and the sky.'

'But…'

'It must be you, Abby.'

The eagles embraced, and the wind gusted above the treetops, carrying its joyful news. Then, a beam of light fell from the sky and settled on the Freedom Tower, and Edgar smiled, knowing that no one could love the Great Wood more than Abby. In her hands, the torch of freedom and opportunity would continue to burn as brightly as it had ever burned before.

That night, music drifted high over Great Eagle Wood, telling of hope and freedom and of a beaver called Bob who had dared to dream. It told too of the eagle who had roused the wind, moved the sky and fought fire with fire. As the Great Wood looked to the future, it was indeed fortunate that such a gutsy little eagle was ready and waiting.